I Am Golgotha

Alan Combes

'The author has a sharp and sympathetic eye and the story is thought- provoking and well-observed. Combes writes with flair and originality.' - Gervase Phinn

I am Golitho is a work of fiction. Apart from actual historical figures, any resemblances to people living or dead are purely coincidental.

Farthings Publishing
8 Christine House
1 Avenue Victoria
SCARBOROUGH
YO11 2QB
UK

http://www.Farthings-Publishing.com
info@farthings.org.uk

Front book cover design by Betton Design, Scarborough

ISBN 978-1-291-57238-4

October 2013 (d)

Crumbling is not an instant's Act
A fundamental pause
Dilapidation's processes
Are organized Decays.

'Tis first a Cobweb on the Soul
A Cuticle of Dust
A Borer in the Axis
An Elemental Rust—

Ruin is formal—Devil's work
Consecutive and slow—
Fail in an instant, no man did
Slipping—is Crash's law.

- Emily Dickinson

CONTENTS

PROLOGUE

The bearded man with the dog at his side leaned on his garden gate. He was watching the new arrival: a man in his thirties, bespectacled, wearing an expensive jacket. The newcomer had parked his car at the water's edge and was carrying a box full of belongings towards the house next door.

Just as he reached the gate, he eased the box onto the pavement and smiled up at the older man who was to be his new neighbour.

"You must be Martin" the newcomer said.

"That's me."

"I'm the new man next door. They call me Richard, Richard Riley."

"Pleased to meet you. I'm Martin."

"I know. The postman told me. I spoke to him yesterday."

For a while nothing more was spoken and the silence was almost too long. Both men looked to the river where the water was as clear as glass. The reflections of trees, reeds, clouds even, were so clear as to induce calm in any onlooker. Time passed and neither man felt it was wasted.

Finally, the man called Martin chanced a question "Is there a Mrs Riley?"

"There is, but we're no longer together. We separated last year. I'll be moving in next door … on my own."

"That's a big property for one person."

"The kids will come to stay regularly. Debra and I share custody. It was an amicable split."

"An amicable split" the older man repeated as though turning it over in his head. "The kids - how old are they?"

"Sammy's just four. Anna's seven. They're good kids. A bit cheeky, as you'll learn, but they mean no harm by it."

"That's okay. I like kids, so does Denise, the wife. Ours have grown up and flown the nest. Some years ago."

Like the river, the evening air was still. Once more words hung around unspoken. Being the newcomer Richard was in need of reassurance. He was not getting it and could not ask for it. Martin, in his world, was thinking hard about how young kids might fit in next door.

Next door. What a strange expression that was in the circumstances and how inappropriate, Martin thought. The well-spoken chap in front of him, with his expensive jacket and designer spectacles, did this guy know what he had got for his money?

"I love the house," Martin said, "so much character. Makes a positive change from estate living. Used to be a railway cottage, I believe."

"Who told you that?"

"Well, you know, to judge from the appearance and how close it is to the old railway line."

On that score Martin decided to say nothing.

"It's certainly getting on. Built well before my house even. It used to belong to Lord Huntley's estate."

"Do you know much about its history?" That was a question Martin found too hard to handle.

"Not much."

Their world went quiet again.

Still seeking reassurance, Richard filled in the silence.

"Have you lived here long yourself?"

"Oh no, not that long."

That was only true if you considered 30 years to be a fleeting passage of time, which, in the history of 'next door', it probably was. What had happened in those 30 years was, in Martin's judgment, best left unsaid.

But now he had learned that there were children involved. The thought made him uneasy. Maybe he should offer a little more by way of information.

"You could always ask Peggy Prince … about its history," Martin suggested.

He was quietly disgusted with himself for choosing the coward's way out and heaping the responsibility on another.

"Who's Peggy Prince?"

"The oldest resident in the village these days. Into her nineties. What she doesn't know about life in Ayton isn't worth knowing. Comes from a family that worked the land round here for… centuries."

"Where will I find her?"

"Over there," Martin said, pointing at a tall chimney that cleared the foliage in an adjacent copse.

"Well, maybe on a long evening when I've got nothing better to do."

We all make promises we have no intention of following through, Martin thought hopefully.

"Oh well, better get set up before dark," the newcomer said, pushing open his gate. Once through the garden gate, he stopped in his tracks and made no secret of admiring the towering twisted oak tree which met his gaze.

"Some tree" he said, summoning a gentle whistle.

"Certainly is. Never seen one like it before. Some say it's two trees," Martin said before turning practical.

"Is the electric switched on?"

"Oh yes. I made sure of that."

Had the new man looked back he would have seen Martin shaking his head ruefully.

"No good will come of that," he mouthed to himself and headed indoors to tell his wife about the new arrival.

*

CHAPTER ONE: *The Builders' Tale*

St Mary's, the church from which I first came, had gradually fallen out of use. In the church's heyday, people had chosen to live at that point in the valley because it offered natural shelter and a point for gathering water. Besides, it was a place of worship and, for its inhabitants, a nearness to God.

There was no need to travel further afield. Most of the people's needs would be met by those who travelled to them.

The River Derwent coursed along the valley and throughout medieval times had supplied blacksmiths with much-needed water for their labours. Thus the place's name: Forge Valley.

Roads were scarcely important in those days. Life was governed more by woodland paths and bridleways. Trails were made by one man following another. There was little by way of planning. Much of a person's waking life was spent following one's feet in those times.

Life changed. People's wants became more sophisticated; their need of spiritual sustenance perceived as less essential. There was gradual movement; new people came to settle two miles down the valley, where the newly-engineered roads crossed and a substantial bridge had been constructed over the river. The river had turned from supplier of aqua vitae into an obstacle to progress that must be forded. By now settlers new to the area had found ways of piping water into houses and bricks and mortar were replacing wood and stone, protecting against the elements with greater efficacy.

For a while those people in the village who were still committed to worship walked the length of the valley to feel secure within my walls. With farm labour declining and the advent of the working week came a demand for worship closer to the place they called home.

Being at a dip in the valley, the old church (that once I was) became permanently cold and damp. It was steeply wooded to my eastern and southern sides and thick foliage on the trees precluded much of the sunlight.

Such an inhospitable building tested the congregation's lessening commitment to breaking point. This was not the Catholic Church that could call its worshippers to duty and rely on their sense of guilt. This was the Church of England and already there was a feeling from its clergy that the people's wishes must be met. The old and needy could not contemplate the long inhospitable journey along the valley and the old and needy had become the stalwarts of worship, as indeed they are today.

Then came the construction of a chapel in the new village and the growing popularity of Methodism. Eventually a point was reached at which St Mary's was abandoned and became a refuge for owls and bats and vermin. Moss and rust corrupted. Parts of the roof fell in at midnight hours, when no one was present to hear or see other than nocturnal creatures. During the summer months, the children of the village, those who ventured that far down the valley, dared one another to spend long minutes in the main body of the wrecked church building or to go in there for a piss, incurring God's wrath. Such daredevil children existed then just as they do now.

Without maintenance, the edifice I had once been crumbled and begged for demolition. But no one seemed to see it.

That is until George Fenby began trundling past on his daily run with horse and cart on the way to his stone yard. He thought the building was over four hundred years old; and he knew it would last only a few more seasons before it crashed to the ground and become beyond recovery.

"There are good building materials in St Mary's," Fenby told his brother-in-law, Ned Ashcroft, "wonderful seasoned timber, quality stone and bricks."

"Too old" Ashcroft said, "Why, the fabric of the whole building will be rotten."

"Not so" Fenby told him. "I looked closely at the building last week when I was watering Jed in the Derwent coming back from the yard. It's stood the test of time, that building. They loved their churches so much in those days only the best materials were used. To do other would have been disrespectful. Pity folk don't still think like that."

George Fenby had an aspect that Ashcroft frequently found annoying. It was as though the top and bottom of his jaw did not meet properly. In truth he could be shrewd and cunning, but this unfortunate malformation imparted a stubborn appearance as though his jaw was set. Thick wobbly lips did little to offset this impression. And the man was constantly in need of a good wash. Ashcroft avoided getting too close.

Pragmatic as ever, Ashcroft's mind was swiftly adjusted; he did not need to think about it for long. 'Owt for nowt' was one of his favourite Yorkshire sayings.

"Why don't we take them – the stones and timber and bricks?" he asked in his usual direct manner. "We could buy some land and build us a house and sell it on for good money."

"We can't take the stuff because it belongs to the church and the law will chase us down," Fenby told him wearily. Normally Fenby himself was the feckless one, but when the subject of money rose to the top his brother-in-law's principles could sink without trace.

"Then why the heck have you bothered telling me about it?" Ashcroft spat out, rubbing a hand across his bald pate where, till recently, a fine head of ginger hair had been. Now his looks and masculinity were in decline, Ashcroft invested in clothing far too refined for a man who laboured for a living. The occasional garish waistcoats and properly tailored shirts betrayed a pretension that one day soon he might rise to the boss class.

"It just seemed a shame to see it wasting away, that's all," said Fenby weakly, "such a waste of wood and stone. It was a mere point of conversation, Ned, and little else. Stuff for an idle moment over a pot of beer."

Ashcroft's dander was up. Why was Fenby trifling with him in this way? Did he take him for a fool? 'An idle moment over a pot of beer.' Who was he kidding? Such moments didn't exist. Whatever did they talk about between the two of them other than work and business matters?

"It's a forgotten church. Who of the modern clergy ever goes out to St Mary's these days? They'll never know," Ashcroft asserted. "We could take it and be gone before a single soul realised."

Now Ashcroft was the one with a point worth making, a very persuasive one, and it gave him some satisfaction to see Fenby stroking his chin, which at that moment protruded in a way that made him look more gormless than ever.

The big land owner in the area was Sir Gideon Huntley, a thrusting young entrepreneur who wished to do more with his life than luxuriate in the style acquired by his well-acquainted forefathers. Huntley dressed in the foppish style that Ashcroft publicly ridiculed but privately wished to emulate.

As luck would have it, Lord Huntley's estate had let it be known that they were looking for a builder to construct a house for the estate's new gardener to live in. His gardener was not yet appointed, but Sir Gideon was determined to make a reputation and rich living through an extensive nursery that was talked about across the county. He had heard of new trees, bushes and shrubs being brought from the colonies. He wanted to establish peacocks and peahens and roe deer and shire horses. When in London on political work he had met William Andrews Nesfield and, many years ago, Sir Joseph Paxton. Their enthusiasm for landscape gardening was infectious.

Fenby had heard about Sir Gideon's plans during a drinking session at The Cock and Feathers. Being aware of his own hirsute and gawky appearance, he did not contemplate approaching the aristocrat personally. But perhaps his more worldly brother-in-law might.

"His Lordship is bringing in big changes. Wants a full-time gardener and housing for workers," landlord Hamshaw had told him and a couple of weeks ago he had shared the information with Ashcroft.

"Could we do that – build a house from scratch?" Ashcroft had responded, letting slip a rare moment of self-doubt.

"I believe we could," Fenby said, "with the materials already in my stone yard and your building know-how we could make ourselves some rich pickings."

"We could use all the materials from St Mary's to build that house on the Huntley estate," Ashcroft said, picking it up. Then he leaned closer and lowered his voice, "That would be one hell of a saving."

"I don't want to get in law trouble – for stealing," Fenby told him, his jaw wobbling nervously. He had had more than his share of run-ins with the local constable, Benjamin Tappett, mainly about drunken behaviour. Tappett made frequent forays to the yard to check that Fenby had done no thieving.

"You are a magpie, Fenby," the portly Tappett would say, "and I trust you not."

How on earth such a tubby man could ever give chase to a villain was a matter of conjecture throughout the village, but the man's arrest rate was quietly impressive. Somehow he possessed a rare ability of being in the right place at the appropriate time. He knows how to get people talking, both Ashcroft and Fenby had deduced.

"Leave the building and the acquisition of the stone to me," Ashcroft said, "but you need to look around for someone who can architect us a house. That is a skill we don't have."

Reluctant as Fenby was to play along with anything proposed by his pretentious brother in law, whom he considered a cavalier fellow, the lure of big money seemed to be the basis of a fair idea.

It was finally agreed that the pair would attempt the building of their first house and Ashcroft was given the job of transporting the remnants of St Mary's Church to his own back garden. For this purpose Ashcroft hired two rogues from the burgeoning village of Seamer a few miles the other side of the river. The youth Makepeace came from a well-known but problematic local family whereas Quibell, the quieter of the two, was an unknown factor. Makepeace had vouched his mate's strength and reliability.

"He can lift a carthorse's rear and he knows about keeping his flap shut tight," was how he put it.

The two youths had been keen enough to accept the purse, even knowing the illegal nature of the work, but it was a different story when they arrived at the church. It was set below a cross roads in a levelled portion of earth at the bottom of Lady Edith's Drive. The wind was up and the moon was down, making for an uncomfortable atmosphere in a derelict building that still carried strong religious overtones. The rush of wind through the trees' heavy foliage was spooky music to their ears. The ruined building being set deep in a valley that was as black as an unlit coal-pit, the easy money seemed less appealing.

“Should we not leave this till the daytime?” Quibell asked.

“Dunce, Tappett will discover us in daylight,” Ashcroft told him.

“Yeah, then we will all be in a dark place,” Makepeace giggled at his own joke.

“I don’t like it,” Quibell added, “It feels like we’re being watched.”

This time Makepeace said nothing and Ashcroft noticed that he was looking out into the night with a distinctly nervy aspect. He realised the two youths were as scared as abandoned children. Ashcroft thought that cheerful encouragement was the way forward.

“Oh come on, lads. I’m a big boy and I’m here to look after you. None of that ghosts and ghoulies stuff. That’s for little lasses. Let’s get loaded up.”

That did the trick. Although it was Ashcroft’s original intention to ride in front of the horse and cart that carried the remnants of the old church, he remained behind for a few seconds as they trundled off into the night. If he searched his own heart he knew he would find the same misgivings that existed in these callow youths, but by holding back they would think him fearless and a master of the night.

Yes, he could see their point. There was something truly unnerving about this place. And for no more than a heartbeat he thought he caught sight of a bluish pallor from behind a clump of trees. ‘What was that?’ sprang to his lips. Best be on my way, he reflected, and mounted his pony for the homeward journey.

Before they began the second run, the youth Quibell said he was 'desperate to piss' and he made his way to the area of the cross roads where the bushes were thickest. Just across the road from where he stood was a cabin with a wattle roof. It was too small to be a dwelling and what was a garden shed doing out here?

Against his better judgement he approached the hut, for hut it was. Before he could get close enough to examine it properly, something moved in the line of his sight. His remaining courage dissolved there and then.

Seconds later, wide-eyed and bouncing like a clown, he returned to Makepeace and Ashcroft.

"I saw her! I saw her!"

Ashcroft did his best to sound tired and unmoved, "Who? Who did you see?"

"It were a woman. Not a woman like of today. From years back. She had a strange hat on with a really wide brim. And an old dress, like really flouncy. And, and, I could smell her."

"What did she smell like, Edwin?" Makepeace asked him.

"Like she needed a bloody good wash," he said.

"You're one to talk."

"But listen that wa'n't the worst bit. It were the eyes. They were starin'. Like looking at you all wild. Like chapel hat pegs they was."

"So what happened? Did she speak to you?" Quibell's friend asked.

"She did not" came the emphatic response, "she just melted before my very eyes. Melted into the night until she was just a part of the blackness."

"Not only that, but there were this building. God knows what it was. Never seen it before."

"Tell me, this building was it small with a door and two windows, a wattle roof?"

"Aye, that were it."

"It was the toll booth for Lady Edith's Drive, yer pillock. Of course you've never seen it before. I bet you've never paid a toll in your life."

"I thought the woman might have come from there," Quibell pleaded.

"So you haven't had your pee?" Ashcroft asked rather heartlessly.

"I'll do it now in sight of you both," and the still-trembling youth did.

By cover of night they made three runs down the valley in order to recover wood, stone and brick. Not one of them let his thoughts dwell on any possibilities outside the job in hand.

An unexpected dividend was the state of two of the window frames on the church's ground floor. They were almost perfectly preserved and, working only by a hint of moonlight, Ashcroft eased them out of the wall with his builder's tools, showing an artisan's patience that was absent from his social behaviour.

"You must carry these on top of our load so they do not get damaged," he told the meaty youths from Seamer.

Despite the indefinable threat offered by the darkness of that place, every part of the old church was stored systematically on Ashcroft's cart.

"If we carry it in the right order and set it down in the same manner as it is, we will have far less trouble when we come to re-use it."

For each run down the valley, Ashcroft, in a scouting capacity, rode his pony a hundred yards ahead in case Tappett should be out and about. The entire operation was only just conducted under cover of night. Dawn was exploding over the coast just three miles distant when the final shipment was laid to rest in Ashcroft's yard.

There was a small copse at the bottom of his own substantial garden and that is where he asked the youths to carefully set down each load. Ashcroft made sure he was in position to rescue the window frames on that first run. He realised that Makepeace and Quibell had been drinking cider during each journey, no doubt to steel themselves against the unnameable threat and so, by the third run, were unlikely to remember his concern for the windows.

He made sure he was there to bully them throughout the unloading and to remind them that if any damage resulted they would receive nil by way of payment.

Then a piece of luck, or so it seemed, came Ashcroft's way. Makepeace, the heavier and stronger of the two youths, had a father that Ashcroft had known in his own youth. This father, Jud Makepeace, was best described as an itinerant labourer. Itinerant, because his well-earned reputation for brawling and thieving caused him to move on from what work he could get with astounding regularity.

But he did get the work; mainly because of his ferocious strength. He could hold up doorways while lintels were fixed in place. He had been known to use his phenomenal strength to hold a wild horse's leg while a blacksmith shoed it. People were afraid and intimidated by Makepeace the senior. He was known throughout the county and even in the city of York as a bareknuckle boxer. His face and ears were misshapen, resembling a hideous rubber mask rather than anything constructed from skin, flesh and bone. His head was shaven and gross fatty bumps erupted all over the cranium. In short, he was a sight for sore eyes.

At this time, the early eighteen hundreds, Jud Makepeace had landed a job with the new railway authority that was pushing into the area and building a line from Scarborough to the market town of Malton and on to York. Through his moonlighting son he informed Ashcroft that he could procure some top quality railway livery at very decent prices.

"What's a decent price, Jud?" Ashcroft asked him, having ridden an old shire horse some five miles for the meeting. It was important to keep a friendly aspect because he knew how easily Jud's demeanour could alter from friend to foe. Jud was used to fear filling people's eyes when they spoke to him, but he saw none of that in Ashcroft and respected him all the more because of its absence.

"For one guinea I can get you enough woodwork for an entire downstairs, Mester Ashcroft…"

"For two guineas could you get me enough for an entire building?"

"That I could…"

Ashcroft asked no further questions. He did not want to be in possession of the ugly facts of how Makepeace did his dirty deals in case Tappett came a-calling and he was faced with an awkward enquiry. Tappett knows how to get people talking, he remembered.

A transfer was arranged. Again Quibell and Makepeace's son were used and the business was carried out on a moonless night. The stock was stolen from the recently opened livery yard in the Falsgrave part of Scarborough. Jud Makepeace used his previous knowledge of the night watchman to ply him with alcohol. He sat one evening musing over old times with him and downing far too much cheap whisky. At an agreed signal, Quibell and Makepeace's son launched an attack, overcoming and tying up and blindfolding both men before stealing the materials. That way any suspicion of complicity would be averted from both Jud Makepeace and Ashcroft.

The operation worked a treat. The stolen livery was stored by Ashcroft beneath several layers of foliage plundered from nearby woodland. The livery was unpainted and as Fenby and Ashcroft intended to develop their own colour theme when they made use of the livery some months hence, Ashcroft figured this greatly reduced the chances of their theft being discovered.

Fenby, the organiser of *Fenby and Ashcroft, Bricklayers,* completed the next part of the puzzle by finding an architect called Austin Lincoln. He had been one of the area's finest, it was said, having worked for rich landowners and landed gentry. Until that is a nagging wife, (they had been denied the gift of children), sent him to the consolation of the bottle. Lincoln was a regular at the Cock and Feathers, where he had a niche respected by all and sundry from the hour of eight till closing.

The night Fenby approached him he was already in an advanced state of inebriation. Fenby had to curb his own disgust at the state of the man: a red round moon face with floppy jowls and dull green eyes that lacked any lustre. This on top of a neck as thick as a jungle vine. When the man stood up he was muscular and squat, quite toad-like. Here was a man on an advanced downward path. Momentarily, Fenby seriously doubted his own judgment, but was eventually consumed by the need to get the job done. The Huntley estate was already calling for tenders. It seemed serendipitous that he had run into this fellow at such a seminal moment.

"Mr Lincoln, I am in need of an architect," Fenby said, approaching him slyly from an obtuse angle.

Lincoln responded by way of a coughing fit that threatened to empty the entire frame of his body of any liquid contents. When the cough had racked his body into submission, Fenby spoke again.

"My brother-in-law, Ned Ashcroft and I have put in a tender for the building of a gardener's house by the weir of the Derwent River on the Huntley Estate. We are worried by the prospect of flooding and would value the involvement, knowledge and experience of a man such as your good self. We need a plan, Mr Lincoln, and you are our best hope. We have sought you out because of your fine name in the field." This last he said through gritted teeth.

Little of this statement bore any truth. For a start no tender had as yet been submitted. Nor had mention been made of flooding between Ashcroft and Fenby, and finally the involvement of Lincoln was pure chance. As for Lincoln's so-called reputation, it was all hearsay. The truth of things was that Fenby had happened to see the man when visiting the pub for a late night drink.

"Didn't the feller over there used to be an architect?" he had asked landlord Bertram Hamshaw.

"You're talking a good 10 years ago, Mr Fenby."

"But he was a good draughtsman, was he not?"

"They say he was the very best. He designed the Millers Arms out at Everly, you know."

That was indeed a testimony to Lincoln's skills. The Millers Arms was mainly a summer pub frequented by the well-off and demanding a horse and trap for the journey.

Following his proposal, George Fenby sat back and waited a good five minutes for a response, but none was forthcoming from Lincoln. Ordering another ale for the two of them he decided to jolly him along.

"So what say we that you attend a meeting tomorrow at my house on Castlegate? P'raps we can all meet up at three'o'clock."

Lincoln made a light moaning noise and then slumped forward. Neither 'yea' nor 'nay' did he mutter.

"So, three'o'clock tomorrow. I expect to see you at 14 Castlegate, Mr Lincoln. I will be there with my brother-in-law," Fenby repeated with volume at the slumped over body, more in hope than expectation.

Fenby went home circuitously by way of his brother-in-law's house. He excitedly told him that his mission was complete – an architect had been found – and that all three of them were to have a meeting the following day.

The Wednesday found Ashcroft sitting in Fenby's living room listening to the clock ticking its way to a quarter past three. At last Ashcroft ceased drumming his fingers and spoke.

"George, tell me who is this draughtsman we are waiting for?"

"He is called Lincoln. He was the architect behind the Miller's Arms over in Everly."

"Lincoln? So that would be Austin Lincoln?"

"The very same."

Without further ado, Ashcroft pulled together the various personal possessions he had placed in front of him – paper, pencils, plans – and headed for the door.

"Ned, where are you off to?"

"Austin Lincoln is nowt but a drunkard and a wastrel, George. I'm surprised at your lack of judgment in this. I am going."

He eased open Fenby's front door and there, standing before him, was Lincoln. Furthermore Lincoln had a large leather case under his arm which appeared to carry materials. The Lincoln who greeted them could do little about being moon-faced and ruddy with hanging jowls, but the eyes were not so lustreless and there was some sense of purpose which communicated itself to the departing Ashcroft.

The truth of it was that Lincoln had retained nothing of Fenby's exhortations the previous night, but Hamshaw, the pub landlord, was Lincoln's brother-in-law. He had overheard the talk and scribbled down the details, passing them on to his sister, Lincoln's nagging wife. Once the drunkard awoke from his alcoholic reverie, it was impressed upon him by his insistent wife that this was an appointment he must keep for money was in desperate short supply and rents were long overdue.

Confronted by Lincoln's arrival, Ashcroft returned to the room.

For two hours the three men scribbled plans and ideas on paper. The basic plan was to use the old church stone as the shell of the building; to supplement it with modern brick on the outside and give it a lime and plaster interior. The animated talk went on into the early hours and finally the three of them shook hands on a deal. What had amazed both Fenby and Ashcroft was the manner of Lincoln's awakening. Everyone said that the world had abandoned the former architect-cum-draughtsman; now this sudden wanting of his skills and abilities had breathed life into the old dog.

The following day Fenby trudged through a foul winter's morning to Lord Huntley's estate office to find a tweedy, ridiculously bewhiskered official of the Lord's and slip an envelope in his hand.

"Mr Fenby, isn't it?" said Huntley's man, Cawthorne. "And what have I got in here?"

"It's Ashcroft and Fenby's tender to build the gardener's cottage on the bend of the Derwent River."

"Ashcroft and Fenby?" Cawthorne repeated, "I never knew that you were a company even, much less a business."

"Newly formed as house builders," Fenby answered rather grandly, "and with our own architect."

Four weeks later Fenby was told he had won the contract, (his price being a good £15 less than the nearest competitor), and soon the walls began to take shape.

Lincoln became a renaissance man and even developed a clever scheme for diverting the river along a lower, wider course to dispel the danger of flooding.

Lord Huntley's steward had been impressed by Ashcroft's building materials and never thought to ask the whys and wherefores relating to their acquisition. Rather than perceiving they came from a church, he thought the materials were those being used in railway properties that were big business throughout the north of England at the time. Indeed, work was about to start on the railway crossing the North Riding of Yorkshire to York and on to Leeds; the passing point would be a stone's throw from the proposed site of the estate gardener's cottage. The livery Fenby had bought through his contacts strongly resembled that favoured by the railway companies, he thought, but considered it no bad thing.

Thinking that the building Fenby and Ashcroft constructed was a railway cottage rather than a house made from a former church was a mistake to be repeated by many over the years. At that time the misconception had the advantage of deflecting any suspicions that Fenby and Ashcroft had been stealing from the Church of England.

Cawthorne met Fenby and Ashcroft where the land had been cleared, adjacent to the river bank. Lincoln was not present. Renaissance man was in a back room of the Cock and Feathers, supping ale greedily and fixing upon his final drawings. It was a glorious May afternoon, the kind of day to put a spring in the step of every man alive.

Studying the building plot and the beginnings of the house walls, Cawthorne, a tall man with a distracting cast in his eye, spoke with conviction.

"This stone will impart a classic line to the cottage, Mr Fenby. I have spoken to Lord Huntley and he is prepared to increase the building sum in order to obtain the very best construction."

So it was that I, the building under consideration, took on my new life; away from religion and the blessings of the clergy. I was beyond the trap of religion and the pointless ceremonies of birth and death and marriage. I was to become a quite distinctive cottage, a home to the kind of people who previously visited me on a weekly basis for worship.

As Ashcroft and Fenby's hired men hacked out my foundations in the weeks that followed, I became aware of the soil's coldness; a coldness caused by the river's proximity. But Lincoln was clever with his proposed diversion of the river. He widened its banks and got the labourers to fill the old course with stone and clay. On top of that, he gauged the house-building work carefully, ensuring that the foundations were significantly above the river's level even in its most swollen course.

Driven by Ashcroft, a harsh taskmaster indeed, the hired hands built me in the space of 16 weeks, spanning spring and summer. Urged on by Lincoln, the two builders innovated and improvised to their heart's content. Foolishly, they abandoned all caution and blindly followed their architect's wishes. The budget became bent and stretched.

Ten miles to the east, near the coast, a local man, Peleg Holmes, had started the production of stained glass. Many small Methodist chapels and Presbyterian churches in the area had created the demand. On his travels Ashcroft noticed it adorning some recently constructed local cottages and thought it would tastefully supplement the stolen livery he had installed. Once a price had been successfully haggled with Holmes, the special glass was commissioned. The decorative glass would appear as smaller panes above the sash windows and as the upper part of the front door frame.

Particularly important was the front door.

"First impressions count for a lot" Lincoln avowed, "no skimping on that part of t'job."

And so it was that they gave him the thumbs up to employ a bespoke joiner he knew who rendered them a panelled front door with a glass window. Holmes ran several designs past Lincoln before he settled on an elongated diamond design.

But Lincoln was as thorough on the basics as he was on the decorative. Stones from St Mary's church were supplemented by modern kiln bricks to the exterior. In many places the walls were a foot thick with the old church stone supplying the inner shell. Flemish brick bonding was imported to the builders' craft on Lincoln's say-so. High up on two of the house's walls white bricks were inserted in the shape of a diamond. That was Ashcroft's idea of an identifying mark. His vision was of a proliferation of Ashcroft and Fenby houses in the surrounding areas, all bearing the diamond symbol.

"This white diamond will be our sign" Ashcroft said to Fenby and Lincoln, "and people will know us all over the county of North Riding by it."

The slate for the roofs was imported from Wales and transport costs caused an intake of breath from the two entrepreneurs, but Lincoln insisted that it was 'the right thing to do.'

"The quality of Welsh slate is known wherever you go" he insisted, "There is none finer."

Outside the property, wrought iron railings defined the garden area at back and front, taking the property to the edge of the path that skirted the river.

By July it was time for Ashcroft to take the window frames out of their muslin wrapping in his garden shed and supervise their installation. The crude temporary window frames were removed then began the work in earnest of replacing them with what had been clandestinely smuggled from the site of St Mary's many months ago. Once that was done, the glazier was called in.

At front and back there was first the main window by which the dwellers could view the river on one side and the wildlife on the other. Adjacent to this main window were smaller cabin-sized windows into which a person might squeeze head and shoulders only. He or she could sit at such a small bay and use the light of day to read a book or undertake embroidery. And, at the top of the window, above the sash, shapes of birds and fish were defined within Peleg Holmes' stained glass.

Fenby judged that such quaint additional features would meet with great approval and he was right. No other river cottage looked quite like this one. Even Lord Huntley himself singled out this feature to Cawthorne when he was taken round the newly built premises, a visit punctuated by harrumphs of 'Splendid!'

Of course, not one of them knew the true function of my window frames during their church days. That was a dark secret known only to myself and to no living man.

"I have not heard of these builders before but we will use them again, Cawthorne," the Lord observed as they stood at the river end of the garden path, looking back at the construction, "They do a good job and are adventurous and resourceful with their materials."

But things had not gone entirely smoothly in the builders' camp. Austin Lincoln had identified with the project so strongly that his plans had gone way over budget. Ashcroft and Fenby, having at last done their sums, realised that they stood to make a greatly reduced profit and therefore could ill afford to pay their architect the sum that had been promised. Indeed, why should they? It was his profligacy that had tipped them into this state of affairs.

All came to a head on a Saturday afternoon in September when the three sat down to review the completed project in the front room.

"Mr Lincoln, we are only able to pay you half the sum agreed," Fenby said. Ashcroft had tried to argue that Lincoln should receive a straight fee of forty guineas and no more, but Fenby thought this heartless. The man had worked his socks off.

"But I have worked longer and harder than anyone asked," Lincoln said, slurring his speech due to a long Saturday lunchtime in the Cock and Feathers. "I have even helped with the construction on days we were a man short."

"We don't question that," Ashcroft butted in, "but you have built in expensive features that were not in our plan."

"And they are the features that will make the house noticed and bring you more work," Lincoln insisted, banging the table. "At a mention by Lord Huntley to all of his rich cronies you can expect plenty more work."

"You may be right, you may be wrong," Fenby told him, "but it's caused us to lose money and made this contract hardly worth the winning," (which was not strictly the truth).

One aspect of Lincoln that Fenby and Ashcroft had never personally tested was his infamous temper. In truth, it wasn't just the constant nagging of his wife that had made Lincoln turn to the bottle. Lincoln had lost so much work previously through his vile temper. His wife's bouts of nagging had come about not just from the lack of offspring but also as a result of Lincoln's irresponsibility in the matter of money.

"I will have the payment in guineas that you promised me and I will have it now," Lincoln said, standing up in the alcove, but wobbling slightly. The blood flooded his features at an alarming speed. Mrs Lincoln would have recognised the danger signals. These men lacked her experience.

"Don't be ridiculous, man," Ashcroft said, "we don't carry money like that with us. We will pay you half of what we agreed and you can receive the money in notes and coins tomorrow."

It was at that moment Lincoln bypassed the part of his brain that suppressed anger and maintained balance. He became a monster with a lion's strength. He rocked and reeled with the drink and perhaps it was this that made the two contractors not take him seriously.

Lincoln made for the cottage doorway where one of the hired labourers had left a hammer the size of a man's forearm on the floor. He seized the shaft, disregarding the rough splinters that flaked off and scratched his forearm. The juxtaposition of a slight, inebriated man and an outsize hammer with which he performed crazy threatening circles produced only mild amusement in Fenby and ridicule from Ashcroft.

"Put that down before you do yourself a damage, man."

With a speed and coordination that belied both his size and his state of inebriation, Lincoln stood directly in front of Ashcroft, raising the hammer above his head. It was hard for the two builders to control their expressions as Lincoln projected a quite ludicrous image. The veins in his thick muscly neck pouted as he stated his case.

"Pay me my eighty guineas now, or I pay you with this," he stated grimly.

Ashcroft, a little too cocky about the power of his own personality, turned towards Fenby grinning.

"Take the hammer off the clerk, George," he said, making his disrespect clear in both word and tone. Fatally, he turned away from his would-be assailant and that was the moment that the hammer crunched down on bone and soft tissue, terribly wounding the skull and finally implanting itself in the shoulder on its downward journey.

The screams of agony from a grown-man are the most resonant, most piercing. The aura that radiated from this terrible act was absorbed by my walls and fabric. This was serious damage to my very heart at just the point where so much had occurred in a past that was beyond the vision of the current occupants. Here was an alcove, a delicately constructed seating point that had been created by men without knowledge of the terrible history of the stone they had used. Now that history had been added to. Could humans ever live peaceably within my walls?

Ashcroft was indeed slain, felled by a single blow. His dying agony seemed to last forever and both survivors, friend and foe, were transfixed. Finally, Fenby fled the building, leaving his partner's mangled frame and the statuesque form of a man who could not believe the reality he had created.

Two local constables arrested a blood-spattered Lincoln that night at the Cock and Feathers. He was taken away to face a jury on a charge of murder that would end in a trial and a sentence from a hanging judge. Ashcroft's devastated body was withheld from the eyes of his widow and children and is to this day interned in East Ayton churchyard.

Killed by a single blow it says on his gravestone, though these days it is barely visible.

*

CHAPTER TWO: *The Gardener's Tale*

The blood from Lincoln's crime was left to impregnate the stone floor. A soldier came to inspect the scene of crime prior to the murder trial, but by then the blood had dried. Weeks passed and not one person came to scour the medal of blood from the floor of River View Cottage.

Nothing is as lonely or devoid of purpose as a house left unoccupied for weeks on end. The elements batter the windows and the bare rooms ache for new life. During this spell men came to mope and measure; searching for evidence and confirmation. On one occasion Fenby turned up with a soldier of high rank, unravelling a tearful account of his partner's slaughter.

Several months went by before Lord Huntley's new gardener, William Binns and his family arrived. The late autumn was by now turning into winter.

The business of Ashcroft's death was hushed up from the wider world but in the tiny community of the village word spread like an infectious disease. A murder done in cold blood by a madman, they said. Lord Huntley told his man Cawthorne not to impart what had happened to the incoming occupant.

"No point, Cawthorne. Only upset them for no purpose. New man's bringing his family – young children. Don't want to cause unnecessary worry. Tell them there was a hitch in the building of the house, but say it's all ironed out now."

Cawthorne sent a man on horseback to the Castle Howard estate with strict instructions. "Tell the new gardener he may move in after another fortnight."

"Why the delay?" Binns asked Huntley's man.

"Been a murder," the indiscreet fellow mumbled, careless of his instructions.

Pop-eyed, Binns demanded "Where?"

"In the new house. There was a fallout between the builders."

"Don't tell that missus of mine," Binns said, aware that he was married to a lady of nervous disposition. She was reluctant enough to make this move away from her wider family. Talk of killings and the like would fettle the move for all time.

Two weeks to the day of the horseman's visit, the Binns family arrived at River View Cottage on a rickety old wagon drawn by two worn out shire horses. William was no horseman and was only too glad to have one of the labourers in charge of transport. Although a thick set man with powerful shoulders, there was a vacuity about Binns' expression that few remarked upon but many were struck by. At that moment of arrival he was apprehensive, deeply concerned as to how his homesick wife would cope and just what awaited them within my walls. He was not unduly worried about the rumour of murder within the house, assigning this to local gossip and exaggeration.

His wife, Amelia, had been a capture for Binns. His few friends had discouraged him greatly when he pursued her in courtship many years ago.

"She is far too much of a beauty for you, Willie, She has a sweet fair face and a body other men will be prepared to kill for," his own father told him.

It was true that her soft downy looks, blonde hair and blue eyes topped a figure that turned most men's eyes, but there was about her an unaccountable nervousness, a quiet anxiety, that seemed to find comfort in William's terse, measured speech. She was relaxed in his presence where all the opposition, the hot young men who pursued her with ambition, merely caused her renewed anxiety. William was her choice and she did indeed make him the happiest man alive… for a short while.

There was another thing about Amelia. Despite the fairness of her looks, she came from gypsy stock. Her grandparents had settled in the area and their children married into the local community. In Binns' eyes, her travellers' roots served to heighten the woman's mystery, the unpredictability of his wife's nature.

Now, as they entered the cottage assigned to Lord Huntley's newly appointed gardener, she emitted a muffled gasp as she caught sight of the blood on the flagstone that had dried to deepest crimson. So strong was the mark that it seemed to demand her attention. She grabbed her children and turned their eyes away from the offending mark. William, despite being forewarned, was equally shocked, but feigning masculine indifference, spoke up.

"Amelia, take the children outside and I'll clean up this floor," he instructed his wife on that gusty early autumn afternoon, “I will put it right. It is nowt, but we cannot have this stain on our lives.”

In human years it was 1858 and William Binns and his young family had taken up the rental cottage that had been Lord Huntley’s promise of almost a year earlier. Lord Huntley, a frequent visitor to Castle Howard, had heard much about the creative gardening skills of William Binns at the Castle estate.

Lord Huntley had made a point of checking the topiary, the flower beds, how glass was used to grow vegetables on a large scale. His enquiries showed that Binns was the man behind this progressive policy. This was the man to fulfil his ambition to establish gardens that would impress all his rich friends. In many ways, Binns seemed a dour, surly fellow, but the results of his labours were plain to see. To Cawthorne, the aristocrat called the man ‘Mister Green fingers’.

In order to impress upon Binns that he would stop at nothing to land his man, Lord Huntley had visited Binns and his wife at their tiny damp mildewed estate cottage.

On answering the knock at the door, Binns did not know who his visitor was but could see by his finery that here was a man of much substance.

Huntley explained his master project and the key role that it was his intention for Binns to play.

He did not belittle Binns’ relative poverty as evidenced by the very basic cottage in which he was housed for that might prove counter-productive, but he did promise him “a more substantial house with a spectacularly panoramic river view.”

"I will commission the finest builders working on this house within the month," Huntley had told him.

Binns was flattered. No one had praised his gardening skills so much, much less a member of the nobility.

He had, of course, accepted Huntley's offer of work although he had to give three months' notice of his departure from Castle Howard. He had been excited and anxious in equal measure during that time but now he had arrived at his new home in this most inauspicious of manners.

Many visitors to my walls have singled it out as a place of atmosphere. All dwelling places have atmosphere, though with many it is understated. Atmosphere is the totality of colour, of light and shade, of mood and temper, of life and death trapped within the walls. Yet still there remains the indefinable, for houses, like people, have souls. There is not just stone and brick and plaster and wood and glass, but the spirit and energy of those who have wrought it. Those who would seek to profit by the buying and selling of houses use the term 'character' generously. Yet they have little knowledge of how such a glibly used attribute is formed. Rarely do such agents rest in silence inside the shell when it is unoccupied and reflect on just what is they are dealing with.

Formerly I had been a church building, but Fenby, Ashcroft and Lincoln transformed that. They subverted my purpose, despite using the materials involved in my original construction. I remained as brick, stone, oak, yew, even stained glass. To these they added tin, brass, copper and modern methods of brickwork and plastering.

From being a spiritual home, a place of repose and prayer, I had become the physical shelter for a family of people, the higher purpose now obsolete.

In the days that followed the screaming of Amelia and William Binns' three children – whether in pain or play – was soaked up by my walls. A house can hurt beyond even what people feel. It can record damage far beyond the limits of human memory. A house bruises and it is said that over years even the glass in its windows can cry.

The reign of terror that marked my days from hereon was no fault of mine. A house cannot assert will as flesh and bone can. I merely reflected what my progenitors (those who built me as a testament to their simple faith) had said about reaping what they had sown. The fading of spilled blood into a mulberry coloured mark on my floor was the doing of man; my only spillage until then had been the flow of skytears from my gutterless roofs. Try as they may, those who through the years scrubbed and scoured this bloody mark could make only the slightest impression.

Sleep did not come easy for the Binns. The baby girl, Letitia, cried incessantly through the time of sleep. One night the crying became screams of terror and the mother, Amelia, woke and sat up firmly in bed. For a fleeting second she caught sight of a pale cornflower blue presence bent over her baby's crib, staring, staring into the baby's eyes. Paralysed with terror, she implored her husband.

"William, you must wake. William, the baby is haunted."

She described what had broken her sleep, the blue-faced 'visitor' who communed with their baby girl, but the gardener thought the nocturnal mirage had been an imagining of his wife. That the shapes she described had been nothing but blue clouds or reflected moonlight: the illusion seen sometimes when the eyes are pressed shut.

I knew the truth. The blue-faced one had been a visitor from the past, but not any past shared by people in this house; a past known only to those who frequented St Mary's, the church which was no more.

"Amelia, you must forget the past of this house and live within its present. This is my chance to make us wealthy, to give us a situation in the world. We have the backing of a Lord.

"Forget the blood we found on the floor; it was not of our doing. We can make a new life here. You are nervous at living so far from your old home and parents. Time will pass. We will visit them soon."

"I will try, William," the wife said miserably next morning, her misery appearing all the greater because of its effect on her fading beauty.

William did his best to personalise their property. The planting and welfare of trees were part of his duties as head gardener on the estate and he obtained permission from Cawthorne to appropriate a few of the saplings for his own small garden. To the north and east he planted horse chestnut and cedar that would grow tall and strong, their thick foliage protecting the house from winds that swooped in off the sea or out of the arctic. Between the house and river he planted willows and right next to the water a weeping willow on which he took a chance for it was well matured. It held firm and, after six months, he was satisfied that it had taken.

On the far bank of the river his men planted a wall of ash and rowan trees. Although this restricted the view across the meadows into the distance, they would provide further cover against the snow and ice when winter was at its harshest.

For his own garden, he took a chance. From the south of England had come a stock of laburnums, chosen by Lord Huntley to adorn the area round his own lawn. With Amelia's help, he planned out on paper how these beautiful trees should be set around Huntley's garden. It was rare that Amelia showed any interest in his work, but it delighted him that she identified with this small adventure. In any case, she was far better, more able, with a pen and paper than ever Binns was. When they had reached an ideal arrangement and translated the paper plan into the reality that bordered the Lord's garden, there was one tree to spare.

"May I have it for my own small garden, please, Mr Cawthorne?"

The tree was released once the agent had spoken to Lord Huntley and Binns spent an entire Sunday doing all that was required to plant it in their front garden.

"You were missed in church today, Willum," Amelia told him, "the vicar gave me a black look."

"One missed Sunday will do no hurt," he said, "Besides, we have a most wonderful laburnum of our own now which will flower golden next summer."

He was right about that, although it was hardly ever to be a golden flower associated with happiness. The experience served to further cool Binns' feelings toward the church. He had taught himself to read and had devoured matter from a fellow called Darwin. That and his observations of the natural world in which he found his meaning served to move him away from the religion his parents had been so insistent about.

One day, later in the year, the son Richard and his younger brother Nathaniel had been happily playing in a beck of the river. So carried away were they with their childish impulses that they quite forgot their parents' warnings.

"I don't like you playing there," the boy's mother told him at supper time, "it's dangerous."

"Mother, we fish with our little nets. Today I caught seven bullheads," Richard told her.

"And I have told you I do not like you in the river."

"Other children go fishing, mother; we make friends with them," Nathaniel, the younger child, said.

"The water's very deep at some points," their father declared, flakes of cheese on his plate, a chunk of bread in his mouth, "Do as your mother bids."

Soon the boys registered at the newly-established village school and their circle of friends grew ever wider. The summer months were best of all and at last the Binns family seemed to have found peace within my walls.

One July day, the boys rushed back from school, dropped their outer coats on the kitchen floor and headed for the beck. Barefoot they waded out to a point where the water was up to the elder boy's knees. He stooped in the water to catch sight of a fish; suddenly he fell forward and hit his head on a rock, stunning him. He was not out of his depth, but his head remained under water for some time. Two or three of his schoolmates grabbed hold of his shirt and trousers and hauled him out of the water. All of which took time.

They lay him on the river bank on his side and water gushed out of his mouth, his lips pouting like a fish's. The boy's father and a gang of three workmen saw the incident from a nearby orchard. The four of them sprinted in the direction of the river.

"I told you to stay clear of the water, boy," Binns snapped, picking up the boy's prostrate body and striding towards the sanctuary offered by my walls. The boy's unsupported head flopped alarmingly as the father rushed towards the sanctuary of home.

As soon as William was inside, he put the boy's body on the floor. The distraught mother bent over the dying child while the father alternately shook and squeezed the lifeless form, trying to force life back into the huddled shape.

There was little that could be done. This was still a time when men believed that death was fated; that the moving finger writes and, having writ, moves on. Resuscitation techniques were unheard of, except by a tiny coterie of those at the medical forefront.

Eventually, all hope of revival gone, Amelia bent over her son and gave his ice cold lips a final kiss; a kiss of death, not a kiss of life.

It was at this moment that it occurred to her exactly where William had laid the boy's body when he brought it in from the river.

"You placed his body on the bloodstain" the mother pronounced.

"I never thought" Binns said, as terse as ever.

Amelia looked at him with betrayal in her eyes, "Richard was cursed by what you did."

Everything went quiet and the three labourers who had remained in attendance, exited the building, abandoning the crushed family. They returned to the village and there spread word of what they had witnessed. That is how legends start.

Mother, father and younger son sat on the floor weeping. From the next room could be hard the daughter, yelling desperately from the baby pen in which she was enclosed.

Each parent thought the other the transgressor in the tragedy. William believed Amelia had been careless in her attention to the boys' proximity to the river; for her part, she believed William had been pusillanimous in his attempt to discipline the boys for playing in the water.

But worse than all this was where the boy's prostrate form had been laid to rest: on the site of Ashcroft's spilled blood.

William tried to be modern and deny that such superstitious practice could have any bearing on the boy's fate, but his wife was strong in the old religious beliefs that had been an integral part of her upbringing in the Howardian hills. A strong belief in witchcraft, ancient curses and remedies still characterised that rural backwater and her gypsy upbringing. But for her husband's ambition her children would have been raised among those hills, away from water and the curse of a murdered man.

There was the matter of the boy's funeral. Although they could not talk about the death itself, both saw fit to decide how the boy should be interred.

"I do not want him burying in the churchyard. These people are not our people," Amelia pleaded.

Binns was not unsympathetic to this position. He had continued to feel that being a regular church-goer was not for him.

"What then?"

"Why can we not bury him in our own garden? Bury him deep and secretly."

"Amelia, the garden is tiny."

"So is our boy. Let us put him in the border and we will plant a tree where his body lies. That will serve to remind us of our lost soul."

Binns knew such a home burial to be against common law, but his wife was right. If they buried him in the dead of night, who was to know?

Two nights later and shortly after midnight, the blade of Binns spade bit deep into the soil. He toiled for the best part of an hour before the neat rectangular hole was ready to receive 'the lost soul'. They could not afford a proper coffin so Amelia gathered together old clothes and rags in which to wrap his body.

The children were put to bed and just father and mother were in the garden. Binns was a bag of nerves, desperate unless some late night stroller was to walk past. Amelia put the clothes on the lawn and then lay Richard's body on top of them. With her fingertips she closed down the eyelids so that he was no longer staring at the moon. From her apron pocket she took two acorns and press one into each of the boy's hands, closing the fingers on top of them.

"What are you doing, woman?"

"My people have always done this with a dead child," she said. Yet more evidence of her gypsy ways, Binns thought, but he offered no resistance. Between the two of them, they eased the body into the grave. Clouds scudded across the moon as Binns said these few words: "You were our first born, Richard. We had great hopes for you, but they have been cruelly dashed. We hope you are happy wherever you are and we promise never to forget you, son." Then, as an afterthought, "Till we all are together again, goodnight."

Was it by intent or accident that he omitted 'Amen'?

Amelia stood watching as glistening with sweat in the moonlight Binns filled in the hole and patted down the loose soil. Then, from his trouser pocket, he took out grass seed and sprinkled it on top. The two of them turned and went indoors.

The whys and the wherefores are irrelevant; the marriage was doomed from this day forth. My walls absorbed the battle cries as their harmony fractured. Soon hateful shouting and accusation were replaced by a frosty silence and a retreat into separate rooms for husband and wife. There was no time from either parent to console the children in their grief of losing a brother.

While Binns' method of dealing with it was to work all hours and spend wasteful evenings in the Cock and Feathers, Amelia took to writing letters home to her parents.

One day Amelia's father arrived with a horse and cart. He packed most of the family's worldly possessions and carried his daughter and two grandchildren away from the scene of their misery. Amelia looked back only once as the cart pulled round the bend. Her last glimpse was of her husband, the Huntley estate gardener, framed in my doorway.

From that day forth, Binns' commitment to his work as a gardener diminished to the point of neglect. He simply lost the mental scheme of things. He could not care less whether plants lived or died. The only watering that vegetables received for weeks on end came from the heavens. What had begun as an exciting adventure that would transform Binns' life from that of a peasant to the possibility of employment one day as a landscape gardener had turned first sour then tragic. Things lasted after this manner for some time. A house does not comprehend time as humans perceive it; in terms of hours, days, weeks and finally years. A house is permanent until man or nature takes it down.

Eventually I could sense that Binns' sense of self-worth had tumbled so disastrously that he was not much longer for this world. Lord Huntley himself had contracted a terminal illness and coincidentally the estate had fallen into disrepair. Binns' poor husbandry since his son's death and the breakdown of his marriage was seen as a principal component in the estate's visible degradation and the managers gave William due notice. It was Cawthorne, the man who had been central to Binns' rise to prominence, who arrived one October morning with the death sentence. Binns saw a malevolence not before apparent in the cast in Cawthorne's eye.

"I am to tell you, Mr Binns, that you are no longer the head gardener of the Huntley Estate. You must vacate this house by the week's end."

"Have mercy on me, will you, man? Can you not see that I have lost my son, my wife and the rest of my family?"

"I am delivering the notice I was commanded to by his lordship, Mr Binns."

"So now you would even take the roof from over my head?"

"I am as sorry as the next man."

"Be gone with you, Cawthorne. This is the house that is to blame anyway. I was cursed from the moment I entered its door, what with its scourge of blood."

Cawthorne looked down at his feet. "By the end of the week, if you would be so good."

In the next few days I witnessed Binns' further decline within my walls. He went to drink and moroseness took over. The day before he was due to vacate the dwelling he sat in a chair for hours and hours. Suddenly, he seemed to find purpose and walked out slamming the door behind him. His bloated body was eventually found bobbing up and down in the mill race on land belonging to Mortimer Prince's farm. At first those who discovered it thought it a heifer that had strayed into the river's hidden depths, so unlike a man's body did it look from afar.

The Huntley estate now fell into a serious state of disrepair. My inner space came to be used as no more than a store – of plants, fencing and tools. The hired hands who worked the estate would hurry in and out of my doors to retrieve whatever they had been instructed to as though I was some kind of forbidden territory.

Word on the estate and in the village was that a curse had been placed on the Huntley lands by the killer of Ned Ashcroft.

Word was passed around that upon his sentencing a half-crazed Austin Lincoln had uttered terrible oaths against the men who had cheated him and so precipitated his murderous act. Before the hanging judge could order the officers of the law to take him down, from the dock Lincoln had embellished upon his hatred sufficiently to include the entire community. Talk of what had occurred at the assizes was conveyed along the grapevine and appeared in the town newssheet. To country folk it explained the downfall of an innocent family and a belief took root that River View Cottage was a place to avoid.

*

CHAPTER THREE: *The Hanged Man's Tale*

I was no longer Lord Huntley's property. With Lord Gideon's demise, the estate's horticultural pretensions ceased. For several months I was uninhabited. At nights the wind buffeted the windows and the timbers creaked with the miniscule shift of the earth beneath the foundations. I was like a deserted ship out at sea; a *Marie Celeste* on terra firma.

An agent arrived one day to secure a 'For sale' sign at the front of the property. The man came indoors with a locksmith to make the doors secure.

"I don't know where they will find a buyer," he said to the locksmith, "It's said by many in the village and on the estate that this house is a house of doom that will bring only misery to those who dwell within."

Perhaps there was some truth in his words. Two harsh winters was the length of my abandonment during which time my fabric was seriously eroded. Glass was broken, seals corrupted and the weakest of Ashcroft's stone and brickwork crumbled.

One February night a drunken vagabond who had been ejected from several nearby hostelries saw the cottage as free shelter. He smashed his way into the property by damaging the rear door with stones and bricks and kicks, leaving it swinging on its hinges.

At first I thought this man a stranger for he was totally changed from the moon-faced individual with hanging jowls who had once inflicted death within my walls. His face had collapsed since those days and his clothing was mere rags. His spirit was as broken as the skull into which he had once buried his hammer.

This was the return of Austin Lincoln. How, you may ask? How could a man who had committed murder and had been sentenced to hang return to the scene of his crime? Hadn't the hangman's noose been placed around his neck?

Following his arrest, Lincoln had been taken to Salford prison and spent two long years languishing in a cell before he was brought to trial. Once a verdict was reached it was determined that he was to be one of the first prisoners to be hanged there. Even then there was much delay before he was brought to the gallows. First there was an appeal that failed then a hangman suffered a heart attack and a replacement could not be found. Finally a new man was appointed and the day of Lincoln's reckoning came.

Incredibly, after fewer than twenty seconds' suspension, the rope circling Lincoln's stout muscly neck frayed and snapped, dumping the semi-conscious killer's body on the drop mat eight feet below. Perhaps the thickness of his neck and the smallness of his person had done the trick. Maybe a more experienced executioner would have checked the rope more thoroughly. Whatever the cause, Lincoln was not hanged by the neck until dead.

At first no one in the prison could believe this sequence of events and Lincoln, after being revived and administered a glass of water, was hoisted back to the platform and the land of the living for a second attempt.

Then came a bellow from down below.

“Leave him” said the magistrate in attendance, “there can be no second hanging.”

The only sign of harm to the disgraced architect was a deep purple weal around his neck. He was administered a second drink of water by the same man who had just minutes earlier secured the rope around his neck with something approaching admiration. As unlikely as it seemed, Lincoln made a full recovery.

He was one of the first men in the whole of England to escape his fate in such a way and in those Victorian times superstition often entered courtly proceedings. It was deemed that fate had intervened because Lincoln was not meant to die in that way. Maybe he was an innocent man after all. Had he not protested that Ashcroft had been unbearably provocative? That he had been ridiculed after completing a punishing schedule of work? That the blow with the hammer was meant as a warning, but due to intoxication his aim had been faulty? That it was something done in the heat of the moment and up to that point he had an unblemished record?

“I am no murderer, your honour. I have never done harm to man nor woman nor beast” he had protested from the dock with due gravity. But the bench had shown no mercy.

“To be taken from here and hanged by the neck until dead.”

The snapping of the rope: was this not God’s way of saving the life of a man who had been wrongly convicted? Besides, he had been hanged according to the judge’s instructions; had the judge said anything about executing the man a second time?

Without further reference to legal authority other than the magistrate's instruction, his jailers turned him out of the prison gate. His hangman even had the temerity to wish him good luck.

Destitute and with only the ragged clothes he feebly stood up in, Lincoln was turned out on the highway. He had to beg, steal and stumble across the Pennines and back to his home village. This journey took many months of tortuous progress and life had hung by a cotton-like thread on more than one occasion. He had even considered living an eremite existence in a Pennine village near Huddersfield, led there by a twisting woodland path. Home then had been little more than a cave; sustenance came in the form of stolen food from nearby kitchens and bins… until he had been chased away by angered locals.

Now he longed to return to his roots. At what had been his former home, he knocked on the front door with apprehension, unable to anticipate how his wife would receive him. Anything could happen. Instead he was confronted by a total stranger. His wife had left the village to escape the shame her disgraced spouse had brought upon her. No one, not even Hamshaw, at the Cock and Feathers would serve him. Until he spoke, Hamshaw had not recognised him, so gaunt and haggard had he become. The last thing Hamshaw expected was to see the return of the bad penny.

"Be out of here, Austin. Thou's not wanted no more in this village."

“Can you not offer me a room for just the one night?”

“And could you pay for it?”

Wearing a sheepish expression, Lincoln propped up the bar.

“Are you out to ruin my trade? You should be dead, man, and that’s the view of every man, woman and child round here.”

Lincoln sheltered the night under the newly-built Derwent Bridge and the next day staggered from door to door begging what scraps he could. People gave not from sorrow or sympathy, (few recognised him) but from intimidation and fear. By now he really did resemble a dead man walking.

Once the scraps of food and the stolen cash had run out, Lincoln chose to return to the scene of his crime.

How could he have considered me, the scene of his most terrible crime, as his sanctuary?

Snivelling whelp of a man that he was by now, he contemplated my door and forced an entry. A broken glass, a fist made of brick and he was inside.

He had escaped the gallows and most miraculously become a free man again, but only to realise that life had not forgiven him. Among those who had once valued him as a member of their community he was now *persona non grata.*

Pathetically, he knelt on the floor and through tears poured out his grief.

“Why was I spared death for this misery? Or is this indeed my hell? Did I really die and am I to be punished by spending forever roaming in misery without home or hope?"

Just when it seems his self-pity had reached its climax he yelled at the top of his voice, "I am in hell" and collapsed face-down on the floor.

Towards nightfall his energy returned. He searched the kitchen and found a filthy wooden mug. He took it down to the bank of the river and there made a show of making it clean. He did not care who saw him now for his mind was made up. He brought back the mug full of river water and a rock taken from the river bed, set them down and went out into the garden. The laburnum had recently flowered and its bright yellow racemes littered the tiny lawn. Lincoln gathered together bracelets and necklaces of these flowers from the golden chain tree and brought them back indoors with him.

He laid the yellow flowers on the kitchen floor, pressing and crushing them with the rock until they were ground into a powder. He paused as if to take courage. After looking up to the ceiling, he scooped together a handful of the golden chain tree dust he had created and placed it with great deliberation on his tongue. He swallowed it deliberately and chased it down with the full mug of river water.

That done, he sat and waited for events to take their course.

I knew that his life had run its course and the man was dying from the inside. That very night the man suffered agonies as his stomach haemorrhaged and he moaned and groaned till the early hours. It was a human life without purpose and by the morning, he who had been spared the normal fate of the hangman's rope, was gone by his own hand.

By the closing years of Victoria's reign, shops had sprung up in the village and the path people took followed the river and came past my front gate. That joyful June morning of Lincoln's demise, a group of workmen, loud and noisy in the crispness of early daylight, wended their way towards the main village, oblivious to the small tragedy that had occurred within my walls the previous night.

A house is without choice in the matter of its contents. This wastrel of a man's corpse was my possession until chance would intervene. I watched timelessly as flies gathered, settling on his lips and brow, burrowing into his hair and skating across his eyeballs. They delivered their cargo and the stripping of the carcase began.

If death was within my walls then outside the world was altogether a brighter place. I sensed birds skipping on my roof, having nested within my eaves and now preparing for flight. The sun rose higher for longer. Warmth and light announced the coming summer. It was in marked contrast to the odour of rotting flesh within my walls.

Days and weeks passed; the smell of corruption still lingered. First rats burrowed into what sweetbreads were available and then mice scuttled about nasal cavities and vacant eye sockets. So much had been gorged by so many.

When what had been a man was reduced to bone, the early summer sun penetrated the special windows that Ashcroft had lovingly restored and those bones became bleached.

One day a bevy of local women paused at my gate, ostensibly to admire the early morning sun's reflections on the river, but each with a wary eye on River View Cottage, as though I might suddenly strike like some living creature. Oh, I was not to be trusted.

The tall gangly one told the others, "This was one of the first railway houses, but the train never actually came this way. Look at the small windows in the corner – they were made for a railway cottage."

Of course, it was not true, but it had now come to be a common belief. The stolen railway livery and my closeness to the railway line confirmed people's expectations. No one recognised the old church within my structure. I doubted they ever would.

"I would not live there for free rent," said the rotund woman, who looked in danger of tippling down the river bank, so unsteady was her stance.

"You would not? Then you are a fool, Edith," said the one carrying a child, "I would not let nonsense stories about hauntings and curses turn me away from the chance of free rent."

"Br-r-r-r," Edith answered back, "a goose just walked over my grave. Stories like the ones I have heard about that place would stop me from ever getting a night's sleep."

So now I knew it for sure. It was said that something evil slept within my walls and those women did not even know at that time about the dead man sprawled upon my living room floor.

During the autumn, a man entered who was so gross that he could barely fit his frame through my front door. He was a mere caretaker, a paid servant of the estate agent who was now my owner. He didn't know that the rear door had been wrenched off its hinges and presented open access.

Even before he unlocked the door I could hear his laboured breathing, his nasal snorts. He was talking to himself as though in confidence.

"Come on, Albert. It's only an old house. Old houses have bad smells. Get some doors and windows opened. Mrs Child said it was a matter of checking whether…my God, Albert, what is this someone has left?"

Albert Freeman, the man who constantly talked to himself, had suddenly been confronted by the bleached skeleton lying, back to the floor.

'Is it real, Albert? Was it a person? Is it a joke?'

Just at that moment, the wind whipped through the rear door and created a draught that disturbed a faulty catch on a side window. There was a sharp slap as wood met wood. To me it was nothing; a house is always flexing its timbers, stretching above its foundations, chafing where there exists a poor fit. To Freeman it was a sure sign that the dead had inherited the earth. He hyper-ventilated, dropped the door key and exited out of the front entrance.

"Albert, you're best off out of here," he told himself.

Albert must have fled to the estate office. More men came the following day in the presence of a vicar. They carried a coffin and after a long hard struggle they pieced together the skeleton inside the box. The vicar was left alone to recite mumbo jumbo over a collection of bones. Every few moments he would give an anxious glance over his shoulder.

A few days later two joiners arrived and fixed the broken rear door before encasing both doorways in heavy wooden frames. No drunken vagabond or chancing thief would pierce the shield that now surrounded my entrances.

It was almost as though they sought to punish me. Without warmth and civilisation a house decays and becomes little more than a monument. I had served as a monument at the start of my days, but at least men invested me then with spirit and meaning. Now I was a home for vermin, my windows a wall of death for careless birds.

*

CHAPTER FOUR: *The Actor's Tale*

Many vacant years had passed since I was inhabited by the Binns family. The Huntley estate had gradually fallen apart, being sold to various farmers and landowners and I was now the property of an estate agent in Scarborough town.

The new agent's boy was tall and fair, as softly spoken as a young girl. Like many who came within my walls, he was a bundle of nerves. With the boy was a man in a black stove pipe hat. The hat was all the more remarkable because it belonged to an outdated fashion. It threw shadow over the man's face, creating a sense of mystery that seemed to unnerve the agent's boy.

"So here we are inside the house, Mr Monse," said the agent's boy, "it was built many years ago by local constructors using local stone."

"There's a not-very-nice smell in here," Monse said in a broad accent, "Can you open t'windows?"

"Of course I can, sir."

The girlish young man attempted to open one of the casement windows, but the catch was too much for him. He looked to the man called Monse for assistance.

"Just leave it, lad. I'll prob'ly do better mesen. Now what was t'price?"

Sheepishly the agent's boy said "I think it was one hundred guineas or the nearest offer."

"Mine is a very near offer," Monse said, "It's one hundred pounds and I won't go a brass farthing above that. I don't do guineas."

The agent's boy was fazed.

"Can I let you know in the morning, Mr Monse?" he asked.

"You cannot. I have another property to look at and I'll be plain – it's more suited than this, but more money. I need to know today, so if you can get yersen back to yer guv'nor with my offer…"

"Yes, but where will I find you?"

"Well, just here, of course. I'll stay in here, waiting for you. I can examine everything while I wait, can't I?"

"You're staying in here – this house – alone, while I nip back to Mr Thwaites?" the agent's boy said with an almost hysterical note of disbelief in his voice. (Oh, I knew then he was as afraid of me as the others, but Monse remained resolute).

"Are you not happy with that? Frightened I'll run away with your house in me pocket?" said Monse, accompanying his words with a big throaty laugh.

"Er, it wasn't that, sir," said the agent's boy, "but you do know they found a skeleton in this very room not so long ago? There, does that not make you nervous?"

"A skellington? Nervous? Me? Look here, laddie, when you've seen the things I've seen in my years you don't take fright at a bundle of bones."

"Sorry, sir. I didn't want to be the cause of an upset," said the agent's boy wondering how on earth this plain-speaking man spent his days that not even a skeleton bothered him.

"Worry not about any upsetment. On your way now and let me know before the day's up," Monse bade him, "I'll be here waiting, but not forever."

As soon as the door was closed and the lad gone, Monse collapsed into uncontrolled laughter.

"Fooled 'em, fooled the lot of 'em," he said, taking off his stove pipe hat and waving it at the room as though anticipating the approval of a non-existent crowd.

What was now remarkable was the change in his voice. The exaggerated northern drawl translated now into cultured tones, every word pronounced with precision. Monse was nothing more than a trickster, pretending to be someone other than his real self. Now something amazing occurred: Monse addressed ME directly.

"Now then, house, you and I could be together for quite some time. You are just what I have been seeking and quite gloriously out of the way. They'll never think to find me here. One way or another, this is a deal I intend to nail."

Two hours later, the boy returned with Mr Stanley Thwaites, the agent, to find Monse impatiently striding to and fro and wearing a dark brooding expression. Plainly, he was not a man who liked to be kept waiting.

"Never let a boy do a man's work, eh, Mr Thwaites?" Monse said, lapsing back into the vernacular and shaking hands on a final deal of £101 despite his 'brass farthing' protest.

Business was concluded within the hour and I passed into Mr Monse's possession.

Monse was an openly expressive man with strange ways, but I did not mind him as an inhabitant for he took no notice of what rumour-mongers said. To him I was a desirable home and he pooh-poohed any talk of dark deeds in my past. The present was all that seemed to matter to him.

The village one mile downriver had begun to expand and young families were moving in. Their children explored the water and in the depth of summer a young girl was drowned close to the beck that had claimed the Binns boy. Monse heard all the kerfuffle on the river bank. He saw the crowds gather as the body was recovered from the water. He was mightily absorbed by the event, but he had no interest in getting involved at the water's edge, much less helping with the recovery. I could see that Monse was a close observer of life, but one who held back from participation.

The man was instead an avid reader. Soon after he moved in a van arrived with large boxes of books. Presumably they had come from his previous dwelling and he greeted them like long lost beings with whom he had formed a close relationship. It became commonplace for him to wander around my downstairs area, book in hand. From some of them he read aloud. Others caused him to pause mid-stride as though they were heavy with conjecture.

Mr Monse bought himself a small terrier and it became a favoured pastime of his to parade up and down the river embankment walking the dog and wearing his black stove-pipe hat pulled down on his brow. Sometimes he even did this with a volume in his hand reinforcing his reputation as the village eccentric. The children of the village, having been warned about me by their parents, ('stay away from that evil house') were now so wary of 'the man in the black hat' that they created a whole mythology round his being and the house he lived in.

Monse knew this tittle-tattle was going on and he seemed to enjoy it, being a man of mystery. Let us put it this way: he played the part. But then, he was always playing the part. None of it was favourable.

Some days he would get up with a resolve to play a part. A soldier was his favourite at one time and he even wore the uniform of a general. He would parade around the house in it and his voice would become stentorian as though he were addressing a hundred underlings. In his mind's eye he probably was.

Then he would suddenly cease and, with a shake of his head, he would return to his own self and address me as an old friend.

"What did you think of that one, house? Were you convinced? Did I fool you that I was preparing for war? Were the other generals under my spell? I will take your silence for approval."

He would play other parts too though he did not always have the costume or the accompanying properties. Once he was a failed doctor, mortified because a rich patient had died at his hands.

Another day he was a spy and spent long hours at the windows observing passers-by and pretending to make notes on their movements. He would talk to himself in frightening secretive tones calculated to disturb any watchers, except there were none.

Once he was secure within my walls, Monse showed a side I had never witnessed in any man. First he dressed in women's underwear, possibly the sort he had purchased when abroad. Next he seated himself in front of the mirror and applied make-up with the dexterity of a professional lady. What hair he had left was pinned up and he placed a convincing wig of golden tresses upon his pate.

Before putting on a velvety green dress with a plunging neckline, his hands explored every contour of his body, as though it was truly a female body and not his own. Oh how he loved himself, dear reader. Each time he did this he paused by the front door, but in the end he dare not take to the street and exhibit himself publicly. This despite the longing to do so that resulted in his making alarming noises of frustration. Human beings are unfathomable creatures everywhere, their secrets trapped behind walls.

Always Monse was trying to explore with great intensity these roles he played. One of his sayings he repeated time and again: "when you play a good man, try to find out where he is bad and when you play a villain try to find where he is good."

But there were times he would disappear for weeks on end and when he returned he would be exhausted, sleeping without thought of the clock. When he awoke on these occasions he would walk about rooms doing repetitive movements full of physical rhythm. Frequently he would talk to me of a man named Brodribb, someone he clearly thought the world of.

"Brodribb says..." would start many a sentence when he was pretending to be another. The identity of Brodribb was to remain a mystery to me. He was never invited within my walls, but sometimes, when Monse appeared to be flummoxed by whatever persona he was trying to adopt, he would say things like "Now what do you think of that, John Henry?" By which I took it that these were Brodribb's Christian names.

On one occasion he returned after four weeks away and he was the most angered and distraught ever. His language was appalling. Until then I had thought him a man of fine breeding whose only trespasses with the tongue had been committed on behalf of whichever character he played. But on this occasion his emotion came from the heart.

"Damned by faint praise" was the mildest expression that came out from Monse. He reserved his wildest excesses for a group of people he called 'the crucking fittics.' He would invite me into his confidence about them, seeking to find solace in his misery.

"Slated by the bastards," he cursed, "I wish them an early grave for they are all ... see you next tuesdays."

Monse lived for many years within my walls. He cursed once when he cut a finger; then he extracted two of his own teeth by tying them to the door and swinging it shut with gusto. This may seem like nothing remarkable except that he administered the cut to himself in the first place and the teeth were perfectly sound teeth in the second. He did these things for the specific experience of going through the suffering. He needed to feel pain because, he said, he must suffer for his art.

Sometimes he would read for hours on end. He lived the stories, reading them out loud, roaring with laughter when it suited and crying like a wild cat for the moon when he was distraught. His favourite author was Thomas Hardy. The man's stories and poems haunted him. They were collected together on a shelf for Monse to pick one out at will. Time and again he would return to a text. It was never a simple matter of reading one from cover to cover and considering it finished.

The one phrase he would constantly repeat during his tenure was 'Character is fate'. He would utter this in apocalyptic tones, usually whilst reading Hardy. Only once did he expand on its meaning. He was drunk at the time.

"Our character determines our choices, our friends. Those we are drawn to and repulsed by. I am a man who prefers his own company. Only Brodribb understands this and yet he has not the time to share with me. What I am to be, where I shall find myself in ten years' time, will be fashioned by who I am."

A house cannot feel sorrow, but there was a terrible sadness about a man who considered himself self-sufficient. After all, he was both the man and woman in his own life. And yet I knew that he was wrong that fate was entirely dependent upon character. For there is always chance.

Although he was often an effeminate, self-indulgent man, the only real softness I saw him exhibit, apart from towards himself, was towards his dog, Mungo. He would take Mungo away with him on his trips and always treated him with tenderness and consideration.

Although Monse announced his moods and concerns out loud and addressed them at me, (yes, it was me he was telling that 'character is fate') it was to the dog that he confided his innermost thoughts.

"Mungo, we are in trouble. It is all going wrong. I feel I may never work again. Worry not, four-legged friend, I will not see you go hungry. You are at the front of my thoughts."

Depression had set in, mainly because work appeared to have dried up. There were no trips for several months. He announced to me "Brodribb has died on the stage in Bradford! Bradford, of all places."

"What style the man had" he told me. "Playing Beckett on stage his final words were 'O Lord unto thy hands' and with that he died of a stroke."

In the days that followed he bought several newspapers, scissoring out the stories and pictures of one Henry Irving, constantly repeating 'I will miss you, Irving. By which I took it to mean that Brodribb and Irving were one and the same person.

So devastated was he by his close friend's death that his own life took the same downward path as Binns' many years earlier.

Yet he rallied and got work entertaining the troops. But rather like a bird that sings its finest song at the point of expiration, Monse was to prosper before the final act. His mood was lifted by something brought by the postman.

"Yes" he said and punched the air once the contents of the letter had been absorbed.

“I am to tread the boards again, house,” he announced triumphantly.

When the end came it occurred during the night. It was one of those occasions that are unavoidable to men. There is a coming together of circumstance that is inexplicable at the time, but appears as some kind of divine or satanic intervention when hindsight is employed.

That night he had frantically packed two bags: one for himself, one for Mungo. Undoubtedly this had to do with whatever had been delivered by the postman. Before his departure though, he turned back to speak to me for one last time.

“We are wanted again, house. The bard awaits, his boards to be trod. I am excited beyond measure. Break a leg.”

Beyond the window the wind had intensified into gale force. The glass rattled and there was a shaking as though the very roots of my edifice moved. Outside could be heard a crashing noise and Monse went out of the back door to investigate. Maybe damage had been done or a tree blown over. I could only stand my ground, fearing what was about to happen.

Monse looked right and left, but his nemesis was approaching from above, not from the side. There are so many unanswered questions. Why, at that tiny juncture in time, did he choose to exit the building? Why did he stand at that particular spot and not two feet to the left or right? The slate that flew off my roof, why was it the leading edge that impacted on the top of his skull and not the flat surface area?

Through the force of the wind and the height of the fall, the normally harmless roof slate was turned into a lethal weapon and it sliced through Monse's skull with deadly precision. His demise was instant. There was not even time to scream at the shock, much less register in his head the injustice of it all.

The slate was his fate. On his life the curtain was drawn.

Not that I was without consequence. The misplaced slate created a hole through which the rain poured from that day forth, insinuating itself into the wood and plaster, storing up trouble for a future incumbent.

There is no telling how long Monse would have lain in my backyard but for the constant barking of his beloved Mungo. By evening of the next day, the barking had become a baying and passers-by on the river front looked forebodingly at the windows, no doubt imagining all kinds of horror within.

A near neighbour, Mrs Imlach, driven to distraction by the noise, asked her neighbour to report the noise nuisance at the police house. The local constabulary, mindful that Mrs Imlach could be a serpent when roused, reluctantly sent out a raw recruit to investigate. Joe Quibell was an enthusiastic but untested 'bobby' who had never seen a man with a slate embedded in his cranium before.

Once in the yard he stood staring open-mouthed at the fallen actor for many seconds before moving on and trying the back door. Of course, it was unlocked, just as Monse had left it.

Poor Mungo was in a desperate state and it says much for the constable's presence of mind that, despite the trauma he had suffered, he was able to offer Mungo a bowl of water. The dog was removed and later in the day several men arrived to carry away Monse's remains.

Again silence reigned.

When life did return to my walls it was in the form of two well-dressed men who packed most of Monse's possessions in hampers. At first they inspected his private papers, looking for proof of identity.

"At least we have something to go on, Lloyd. This calls for a day's work at Somerset House."

"And who'll pay the bills for my time, that's what I want to know," Lloyd quizzed.

"Whoever the new owner of this is," the other answered, throwing up his hands to indicate the full expanse of my building.

Many weeks passed. The wait was excruciating. One day the front door creaked open and the stale May air was offset by the sharp tang of a woman's perfume. Mary Ford was in her early thirties. She came with an endless supply of bags of clothes and boxes of books, but nothing could conceal the nervousness she felt moving into River View cottage.

Mary Ford would have been considered beautiful by most men. She was tall and dark with an accompanying fragrance wherever she went. Her eyes were wide and constantly searching; her most attractive feature. She wore loose-fitting clothes that hid an almost painful thinness; the average man could have encircled her waist with his open hands.

She was constantly looking around once indoors. The only available light at that time was supplied by nature or oil lamps that threw disturbing shadows on my inner walls. I knew that she could not continue like this – a bundle of nervousness and anxiety.

Within days she had made an important decision. She called in the electricity people to wire the building. A gang of four men came and chipped and chiselled into my walls, running cables hither and thither. Candles and storm lanterns were soon made redundant and Mary Ford grew braver within the walls once bulbs were illuminated.

The modern conduits of energy and light they constructed brought unaccountable change. I was now a far cry from those days when worshippers huddled within my walls. Not only were these walls able to absorb, now they could convey messages and signals. I was alive and carrying impulses through my very fabric.

For Mary Ford, (I learned her name because she frequently addressed herself aloud as though to inspire courage; in this action she most resembled her dead uncle), was Monse's niece and had inherited his property. The illumination of the building came as a visible relief to her. Still she was twitchy and uncertain, but the ability to throw light into a room before she entered clearly emboldened her.

Mary Ford was a teacher in nearby Scalby and each day a taxi arrived to convey her to the school. At night she would mark the children's work and constantly remark to herself upon its imperfections.

"Samuel Perkins, when will you learn to use a capital letter properly?"

"Thirty one add sixty two is not ninety four, Emily Dawkin."

Nothing, however, could have been more marked than the contrast between her uncle's dour and lengthy silences and Mary Ford's constant chatter to herself. Monse may have addressed the world, but more often he observed lengthy and painful silences in which he practised bizarre expressions and eccentric body movements.

Sometimes Mary Ford spoke out about her Uncle Edward (Monse) and I gathered he was her mother's brother and at one time had been a significant player in London theatre and provincial repertory. However, there was no hint of fondness or sentimental attachment on the few occasions she spoke of him.

For three years Mary Ford ploughed a lonely furrow. Occasionally she would invite fellow teachers to join her at the house for tea or an evening of cards. Mostly her time was spent marking books, preparing lessons and reading.

One evening she arrived at the house with a new lady friend, an accountant by the name of Miss Joan Groves. The newcomer sported a hairstyle known as the Eton Crop. The cut was stern and directed people's focus to the face and the shape of the head. It was a style associated with the boys who attended Eton School but had been adopted by fashionable young women. Clearly, Miss Groves belonged to a new style of self-confident female that sprung up during the 1920's and 30's.

Joan Groves was Mary Ford's lover and just before Christmas she moved in with her. Once again my four walls were the subject of stories amongst the village people, many of whom thought lesbianism was confined to distant civilisations like the Ancient Greeks. The ordinary people of the village believed it was the influence of where they were living that had led the two women 'astray', for we were in a time when no 'normal' people indulged in homosexual relationships – at least not publicly.

O how my floors creaked and my beams lurched the night after I heard Mary and Joan discussing this topic with much laughter. They were unmoved by the wild speculation about their love affair and found it quite fascinating. At least I could sense that Mary Ford's constant anxiety about the dwelling was now under control. The two lived in harmony for a time that made it as settled within my confines as any since Ashcroft's murder.

There was another thing about the Groves woman though. She knew. She was on a higher plane than others who had lived within my walls. Mary Ford could not see the frequent glances her partner threw in the direction of the casement windows. For a self-possessed woman who was bursting with confidence, those occasional moments betrayed unease. She never pulled up a chair to either of the smaller casement windows even though she read often and light from outside would have washed over her book.

"What's the matter, Joan?" Mary Ford asked her following many days of near silence.

"I am not well," she said, "it's hard to explain."

"Is it the flu? I've heard it has come as far north as Yorkshire."

"No, no, it's nothing like that. It's to do with…" Instead of completing the sentence, she raised a hand to her brow, touching one side with her thumb and the other with her index finger.

"You have a headache?"

"Oh, Mary, if only it was that simple."

"Well then you must explain, because I have no idea what troubles you."

Instead of facing up to Mary's enquiry, the Groves woman went off at a tangent. She could not find the courage to tell a rational person that she was overwhelmed by an atmosphere, by a cold spot within a room that was heated. Indeed, that she felt looked upon.

"I am tired of always having to go outside for the toilet," she said at last. "Some nights when I am forced to go it's like being drenched by buckets of water."

"There is a plumber who serves the school where I work. I could ask him to take a look at our situation," Mary said.

"Oh yes, please, I will even pay for it myself."

Mary Ford duly contacted the plumber; a young man of immense good looks. He was skilled at his work and I could see that his attention was captured by Mary Ford. Did he know the nature of the relationship between the two women? Either he did not, or he did not care, for there was a confidence and arrogance about this young man. He was blonde and tall with a fine set of teeth. He laughed loud and long as though he was enjoying every minute of his young life.

Why should he take village gossip seriously when his classic good looks turned women's heads wherever he went? What Henry Newton wanted, Henry Newton got.

The plumber carried out most of the work during the long summer school holiday, plumbing in an internal toilet and closing off the outside facility. He would visit the home on a regular basis, secure in the knowledge that Joan Groves was immersed in figures and company law in her office job while Mary enjoyed the long summer school vacation. Of course, he tumbled into bed with Miss Ford, leaving her lesbian lover out in the cold.

The laughter and lust between a man and a woman that echoed within my shell were unfamiliar sounds indeed. Sadly, I knew such joy must be the precursor of misery. It is always the same with humankind.

So it was that after love-making one Saturday afternoon, Mary Ford lapsed contentedly into her pillar, only to look up and see a spreading patch of grey-green mould.

"Ugh, Hen-ery, what is it? What is it?" she squealed, as though it might have been a giant spider.

"Thou's got damp," Henry remarked, "and it'll need seeing to."

It took him a week to get round to it, but he ran a ladder up to the roof and found the spot where the projectile that claimed Monse's life had launched itself from.

I could only think some good of the man now, for at least he had shown concern for matters beyond his own little life. He even found a plasterer friend to make good the internal damage.

I believe Miss Groves sensed that her time of emotional content was drawing to a close. She threw even more intense glances at my casement windows during this time. Rather than seek a showdown, she settled for material comfort and the acknowledgement that never again would she and Mary be close. She was, after all, a mere lodger in the house so hardly in a position to protest whatever she feared might be going on.

With Mary Ford's blessing, Miss Groves began a project. In the world at large, a terrible conflict had broken out and monstrous birds with payloads crossed the waters between Britain and the continent. Declaring the outside toilet redundant now they had internal lavatory facilities, Miss Groves sought to turn it into a small air raid shelter, one that would ensure the survival of Mary Ford and her. She brought in a local builder, Herbert Ashcroft, who claimed his great grandfather had built the house many years ago before his tragic death.

"What a clever idea, Joan, to use a lavatory as a bomb shelter. No one else would have thought of such a use," Mary Ford congratulated her.

But gradually the truth dawned on the woman with the Eton crop that Mary Ford only wished to survive the war with Henry Newton, the plumber. Joan Groves had found letters and heard whisperings which made her feel superfluous to others' needs and unlikely to meet another soul mate. Her sense of isolation within my walls increased her feelings of unease. She knew there existed something in the building that disturbed her profoundly even if she could not name it. Gradually she began to feel that the accountancy work she did was without point. Passionless numbers that attached themselves to lives she neither knew nor cared about. Indeed, who cared? She did not anymore.

She bought the rope at the hardware store in Scalby where Henry Newton, the plumber, worked. It gave her a perverse satisfaction even though he was out of the shop on the day of her purchase.

She took a day off work when the school was on half-term and the lovers had used the opportunity to have a secret tryst. With a final defiant glance at my casement windows, she strode across the yard and entered the old toilet with its now reinforced roof. She suspended the rope from a beam that Ashcroft had inserted into place and used an upside down industrial tin as her launch point.

It was several days before the body was found. The news that Henry Newton had been called up and was to be posted to Africa for the war effort had left Mary Ford in distress. She lived for several days in a world of her own until it occurred to her that she had not seen her lady friend for some time. But where would she start enquiring about her missing partner? Enquiries to Groves' employer produced just as much head-scratching at the other end.

"We thought she must be at home ill," Mary Ford was told.

"But I haven't seen her for… for days."

What had happened to the normally reliable, Eton-cropped stalwart of the accounting office?

Eventually, it was the smell that led Groves' former lover across the yard.

I heard the screams outside my walls and absorbed the grief as Mary ran about the house in hysterical postures of disbelief. Those screams and wails reverberated and continued to echo down the years.

Of course, the death of Joan Groves would not only terminate Mary's tenure at River View Cottage, but bring to an abrupt end her love affair with the plumber.

*

CHAPTER FIVE: *The Taxi Driver's Tale*

Joan Groves had been a smoker. The evidence of that lived on long after her death. Mary Ford's tasteful decorating, applied during school holidays, was tainted and yellowed by the smoke emitted by her former lover's habit. Sometimes, given the right conditions, my walls would yield up those same tobacco smells, months, years after. Inhabitants would stop in their tracks. No one was visibly smoking yet the odour was clearly present. It was as though a practising smoker was in the vicinity.

'Was this the ghost of some long dead smoker, one who used to live here?' I once heard an inhabitant say many years later.

The residual effect of tobacco smoke is no more startling than that of grief. Intense passion does not simply bounce off walls and disappear into the atmosphere. It becomes trapped in the very fabric of buildings. The right conditions can trigger the memory of such intense feelings, restoring them to an effective state for those who are sensitive to atmosphere.

One day, after disappearing from the village for several months, Mary Ford returned, bringing with her two men from a removal firm to help pack her belongings in two sizeable trunks. Evidently, it had taken her time to work up sufficient courage and control to return to the scene of such pain.

In an upstairs cupboard, secreted away many years ago by Mary and Joan were her long lost uncle's books, in particular his proud collection of Thomas Hardy novels. Her own books she had always kept apart from Manse's and she had taken them to her new address, about which she did not speak.

"What shall we do with these, miss?"

"Do as you like. Their owner is dead. Build a bonfire with them for all I care."

The two men looked at one another with surprise. Neither was of a literary bent, but most of these books were leather-bound and surely worth something at one of the auction houses in York or Leeds.

"Er, what about if we take them for ourselves?" one of the chaps said.

At that moment Mary Ford was scrubbing the sink area of the kitchen. She paused and turned to face the questioner. Her expression was soft and thoughtful and he thought she was about to consent when suddenly there appeared a meanness about her mouth. She seemed to reflect on the pain that her stay at River View Cottage had brought her. It had occurred to her that her wayward uncle and his possessions were in a large part responsible for the tragedy that had befallen her.

"No, you may not take them," she finally said. "What I want you to do is burn them all on a bonfire. Do it now. On the river bank between the footpath and the river."

The removal man looked with disbelief into her eyes and saw only conviction and certainty. Within the hour, the man and his companion were, with heavy heart, loading a bonfire with fine books that would have brought a small fortune at auction.

Passers-by looked on with incredulity; never before had the rural calm been disrupted by such a strange gathering: two men firing books of fine quality on a lush river bank goaded on by an intense woman.

Once all her remaining belongings had been gathered, she did not even look back as she stepped out of the building for a last time. Her final expression was unforgettable. She looked back at what had been her home for a number of years with fear and not a little loathing. In her eyes River View Cottage had become a monster, a beast that had threatened her very humanity.

Once again my walls were cold, my fires unlit, the creaking of my boards unheard. The presence of people, by which a house is defined as something greater than a mere building, was absent.

Meanwhile the war had run its course and everywhere people were adjusting to the promise of peace. New houses were being built and occupied, but no one local would take a chance on a building with my tarnished reputation.

From afar, Mary Ford had no option but to ask her agent to accept tenders for the sale of River View Cottage. It was beyond consideration that she dwelled within the building awaiting a prospective buyer. She wanted away for the associations were too powerful.

On the last day of March that year, the front door creaked open to reveal Sidney and his young bride. At his joyful insistence he carried his bride across the doorstep, which he called a threshold.

"Let's do this proper, my love."

"Put me down, Sidney. This is silly."

"It's not silly, Popsy, it's what men do when they love their wives and want to make a fuss about carrying them into a better life."

This was a brave sentiment for it was true that Sidney, a relatively small man, swayed unevenly with the frame of his bride. He had been drinking quite heavily and Popsy's arms and legs stuck out in ungainly fashion while she rested in his arms. She loved her special name of Popsy for neither she nor Sidney liked the name Pauline that she had been christened with.

"But you'll drop me and it'll be a hospital job," she gently protested.

"Don't underestimate my strength, Popsy. I learned a few tricks while I was in Canada. Besides hospitals will be free soon."

During the recently-ended war, Sidney had been posted to Canada, where his duties had largely been concerned with the packing of parachutes; he had coped with loads of considerable weight and size. What was his pretty young bride compared with a pack of two dozen parachutes moved from plane to plane?

Whilst living abroad he had developed a gambling habit in a couple of small-time casinos in Regina, Saskatchewan, where he had been posted. With a small group of friendly Canadians he had caught on quick in several small poker schools, making a tidy fortune. His popularity had been aided by his film star looks. Although only small in stature, he possessed a magnificent head of jet black hair that culminated in a widow's peak and dark brooding eyes. Later in his life he was to be described as a Dirk Bogarde lookalike. His success in the casinos, where he had become a much-favoured limey, resulted in him arriving back in England with a tidy little nest egg. With this money he had tendered the bid that purchased River View Cottage.

The long barren spell when no life had inhabited my walls looked to be over and for that I was thankful. At last here was a couple that promised a time of contentment, happiness even. Sidney had spent the winter months painting, paper-hanging, plastering and plumbing. Although not a skilled man by training, he was resourceful and afraid of no challenge. Such men are to be admired. I felt he belonged within.

Popsy, his bride, had shown no such commitment. She was quite a tall girl; certainly a few more inches than Sidney. Her eyes were the brightest blue and although she could purse her lips in a quite threatening manner, her dimpled smile won most people over. Always she was generously coated in memorable perfume.

The house had been Sidney's choice. She frequently visited him in the day time during this preparation period, never stayed long nor offered to pick up a paint brush or prepare a pot of tea. And she never remained beyond the daylight hours.

In many ways she was reminiscent of Amelia Binns: attractive, shy and, within my walls, somewhat gauche. She never moved about the building as though she belonged in it.

But Amelia had her children to occupy her. For Popsy there was no such distraction. Sidney once said "This will be a good place to bring up our children."

"Oh it will, will it? And how many of them are we going to have?"

Sidney gave the strangest of answers.

"Why two, of course. One for you and one for me!"

"Ha-ha" she said in a most disparaging way.

At first their love-making was tender and fulfilling. Always their passion started with Sidney lying on top of the bedclothes behind her. He would cup her breasts and enjoy the sensation of his 'rod of steel'(she chuckled every time he called it that) making contact with the soft skin of her buttocks, rising, slowly rising. When he was good and hard, he would flip her over with all the strength that the years of parachute-packing had given him. Then he would mount her and she would beg him to be slower and gentler so that she could feel every stroke, but often he would surrender to his instincts and push-push until exploding into her and grunt like something inhuman.

Their love-making in that first week followed a nightly pattern, but by the second week there was a change. At their most intimate moments, her eyes were focused on the corners of the room. She felt as though she was being watched. She could not have said by whom or by what, but there was a definite sense of not being alone in the room.

One night as he was about to start his thrusting she stopped him, putting her cold hands on his biceps to restrain him.

"What? What do you do that for? God, you feel so cold."

"The smoke, can you not smell it? Tobacco smoke. Like someone in the house is smoking."

At that time neither she nor Sidney had indulged in the habit.

"It'll be somebody passing by," he told her impatiently, "the smoke's drifted in through the window."

"The window's not open."

He stopped and disengaged, frantic with disappointment. "Look, Popsy, there is only me and you in *our* house."

"I can't relax."

He realised it was hopeless and offered to go downstairs and double-check for intruders. She accepted his offer despite being confident that he would discover nothing. But the sexual arousal had deserted her and she was glad of an excuse to call a halt.

When he left the room and her only awareness of his presence in the same house was the soft thud of his footsteps on the stairs, the fear in her eyes was stark. Her imagination took over and terror stalked in the darkest recesses of the room and of her mind. The whites of her eyes pulsated in the dark for incredibly she was such a prisoner of the fear that she dare not even get up to switch on the light.

He was away downstairs much longer than could be accounted for. Had he found something – a presence – and had something happened? Had he gone outside the back door to check? None of these things, for he returned with two cups of tea that he had made, an effort at low grade domestic bliss to restore harmony.

Yet the following night was as different again. They carried on as I had never seen inhabitants behave before. He took her before they were actually ready for bed. She was undressing in her normal somewhat sedate manner when he attacked her almost viciously. He grabbed a breast in each hand very firmly. He didn't seek to hurt her but nor was he especially gentle or soft. It seemed she would cry out in pain, but instead she reached down with both hands, cupping his balls in one and grasping his rod of steel with the other. He was shocked and thrilled. Nothing like this had passed between them before. In response he moved his left hand from her breast and planted it between her legs, stroking sensitively until she was wet.

Both Sidney and Popsy were transported to a realm they had never occupied before, for living within the walls of River View Cottage had turned them from civilised beings into animals. Soon they forsook the bed to roll and wrestle on the floor; grunts, sighs and shouts taking over from language and whispered confidences. When they had climaxed and it was all over, both were amazed at the state they had briefly inherited. While Sidney continued to breathe heavily with the thrill of it all, Popsy was in a state of shock and now the fearfulness was of what the house seemed to be doing to her.

Did she really believe that a mere building could harness the power to determine the sexual drive, the emotional mood of its inhabitants? It would appear so, for from that day forth I became a battleground and not a love nest or even a place of refuge

To make matters worse her new husband had taken a job as a taxi driver. He'll never be home in an evening, she convinced herself. Driving was another skill Sidney had picked up in Canada. He thought it an excellent way of making a living. It was a skill easily mastered and gave him ample opportunity to practise the social skills he prided himself on possessing.

Since Victorian times Scarborough had been a seaside resort, but with peace restored after the Second World War and the railways going through a period of expansion, the town had become a focus for summer holidays with the new working classes. Sidney's lot was to sit patiently outside the railway station awaiting his fares and running them out to the various holiday destinations.

Often he would work the late shift for then people were plied with alcohol and the tips were far more generous and loose coins tumbled down the taxi's back seat: a repository for carelessly lost change. So full of pride at his bounty was Sidney that he completely failed to notice the terror that had taken root behind the eyes of his bride by the time he returned at the midnight hour.

Popsy regretted now standing by while Sidney had settled on his house. If only she had played a more active part at the time of choosing, she found herself thinking. Yet when she tried to rationalise it, there were no words or images to justify the fear.

I am a mere house. I do not talk or whisper dark secrets or produce transparent images or deceptive illusions. Yet she would feed her fear, this Popsy, with the few inexplicable noises: the occasional crack of a joist, the settling of a window frame, occasionally a careless bird flying out of the upper branches of the oak only to thud sickeningly against the glass. None of this meant that she lived in a house full of demons.

Of course a house will move and imperceptibly change. It is not a cast iron edifice rooted in marble. A house is made mostly from pliable materials resting on malleable earth. To this extent I am a living thing and must be accommodated. I am a home too: a resting place for the echoes and the waves and the energy that have been a part of me from my beginnings.

The lovemaking between Sidney and his bride came to an abrupt end. What had he done wrong, he asked her. She told him the love was turning to hate because of this place.

"I don't understand why."

"I feel I'm being watched all the time."

"Don't be silly, Popsy. Watched by who? Have you seen somebody at the windows?"

"Watched from inside, not outside."

"You what?"

"That night, when we were making love and it got … out of hand. It scared me."

"But you were as much a part of that as me."

"I know, I know. I'm not saying I wasn't. But it was like something was firing up the animal part of me, turning me into a…a beast."

"You're being silly."

"I've never felt like that before. It has to be something about this house."

"Next you'll be telling me it's haunted."

What should she say to that? Had she some special insight? There was a sadness in the air like the realisation that a wonderful dream would not come true.

"This house...it's not for us," she said.

"But my sweet Popsy" he said "this is the house we chose. This is where we want to be."

"No" she said "WE did not choose. This is where YOU wanted to be."

"But I thought –

"You never bothered to ask though, did you, Sidney? You went ahead and assumed."

He was shocked, deeply shocked, because I was his dream yet now he could see that his dream was not a shared thing. It was a rude awakening for he had set his mind on a wonderful Christmas with snow decking the river bank and the waterfall twinkling with the weight of icy water and the sharp frosty wintersun.

And now – after less than four weeks – she was leaving him. Could he not see it even through his desperation?

"What if I give up the taxi driving? The quarry has opened up Cockrah Road and they're hiring men. That way I will be home at night. You will have no need to be afraid."

"You love the taxi job."

"I love you more."

"This house can never be right for me."

But the image of the house he had paid for with his Canadian adventures burned strong in Sidney's eyes. To him I was proof that although coming from a humble background he could achieve, proof that he could make something of himself. He had offered Popsy compromise, but he could not offer her surrender.

"You haven't given it a proper chance" he pleaded desperately, "less than four weeks. That is no time."

"It was all I needed. I will never make this house my home. It cannot be."

She let a silence develop in preparation for the bombshell she was about to drop.

"Tomorrow I shall pack and leave for a new place."

"A new place? Where is that?"

"On the seafront where I have always wanted to live…if only you had taken the trouble to find out."

"The seafront in Scarborough?"

"Filey. It is less vulgar. More open. I shall not feel hemmed in."

"You have a place in Filey but never even told me?"

"It belongs to my brother. He rents it out. Right now there is no tenant."

"All this has been going on behind my back?"

"You were not listening, Sidney. You were in a world of your own. This house had taken you over."

It was preposterous – a marriage that had not even seen the month out, but he could not think what more to say.

She was no longer bitter for she was now set on a course of action that would improve her life.

"Don't blame yourself, Sidney. It's the place's fault. One day you might see that. My brother has arranged transport. He will pick me up at six. I'd rather you weren't here."

There was no more to say. She left that morning for work, leaving him alone in the house for his shift did not begin until 2 p.m. He thought he would have a light lunch in the pub rather than sit at home nursing his misery.

The road between River View and the Cock and Feathers was now filled in with new development. Houses, most of them made with Yorkshire stone quarried nearby, lined the way. Notice had been given that the railway from Seamer to Pickering was to close down and the track replaced by an asphalt walkway. The station yard was in the process of being turned into a holding bay for the council's highways department. Everything was in a state of change and on top of everything else it unsettled Sidney.

In sight of the Cock and Feathers there was now a butcher's and next to that a slaughterhouse. The scream of cattle about to be slaughtered was audible and Sidney covered both ears.

Once in the pub, it was Dot, Hamshaw's missus, who served him. He bought a milk stout, figuring it would help his stomach, which had been turned upside down by the morning's events.

He sat down in the bay of the window. Everything crowded his mind. Was she right? Could it be that River View and its surroundings were changing from the ideal he had invested in to something more urbane and threatening?

How much did he want her back, that's what it boiled down to. That and whether he had burned his boats with her. He supped his stout with great deliberation. He became aware of Dot watching him from behind the bar.

"You all right there, Sid? You don't fancy a cheese n pickle sandwich? I could knock one up, you know."

He liked that, being a member of the community, people knowing his name. Why couldn't Popsy have appreciated that? He consented to the sandwich and kept his eye on the pub clock so that he could catch the 1.30 bus to town where he would pick up his taxi for the shift.

He was not back at the house at six'o'clock when presumably she returned with her brother to pick up her stuff. It was half past midnight when he returned and to him I seemed empty, like a place in mourning. Foolishly, he had arrived home from the shift with his heart in his mouth desperate to find that she had had a change of heart and was staying with him after all.

He decided to tell nobody about their separation. The embarrassment he felt at being half of a marriage that had lasted less than a month was sufficient to seal his lips. Besides, he knew that Ayton (which was by now split into East and West) was small enough for word to travel at speed. The rumour would take care of itself.

Not for the first time, River View was home to a single male. But Sidney was distinctly more committed to his living quarters than Binns or Manse had ever been. I was his investment and he was one of a new breed of men who saw their houses as a means of self-expression, to paint and decorate, to renew and rejuvenate, to mend and extend. It was these activities that accounted for most of his energies over the months that followed. Work and home seemed to be his life until late one September afternoon he came home with a fellow taxi driver, one called Gerald. From the trunk of the car they carried in a modern record player and a stack of records called 78's.

Gerald was so excited by the possibilities offered by this gramophone and the large plastic discs that carried songs, happy and sad, that he twisted and cavorted like a young child at Christmas time, communicating his enthusiasm to Sidney.

Indeed, the two of them danced together and this embarrassed Sidney, even though Gerald was only trying to teach him the correct steps. Sidney insisted on drawing the downstairs curtains in case passing folk would think there was 'something going on'. At this Gerald tapped him playfully in the ribs and asked what if they did and accused Sidney of having 'two left feet'.

"I'll tell my Shirley what you said," Gerald jested, "making out I'm a queer."

They quickstepped and foxtrotted until the pair of them were quite breathless. This was the most fun Sidney had had since Popsy departed for Filey and he thanked Gerald for bringing lightness and laughter back into his life.

"So why don't you join Shirley and me at the Spa tea dance this Saturday?" he asked.

"Because I'll be a gooseberry and won't know where to put myself."

“Rubbish” Gerald barked, “There are plenty of single men and women who go. Time to start rebuilding your life, Sidders.”

It was with great reluctance that he finally agreed to join them at the Spa ballroom.

“It’s a masquerade night,” Gerald informed him, “You’ll need to get yourself a face mask.”

There was a costume hire shop in Bar Street in Scarborough which had an array of masks and he settled on an unusual black diavolo devil venetian mask. It looked most menacing the way it curled into sharp prongs at the bottom and gave a hint of devil’s horns near the hairline.

He adjusted it several times in front of the mirror near the front door in River View before leaving the house for the ball. At first it amused him, but after a few trials he felt a strange fear at the mirror image that confronted him. For a few seconds, no more than that, he lost his sense of self and thought the horned one was present in the house with him. His heart beat feverishly and he had to rip off the mask, turn swiftly on his heel and check that no other was present. It was only momentary, yet it was to prove a significant event.

Gerald had not exaggerated; the ball was awash with singles and soon he was attracted to a girl who wore a cat mask of a green velvety texture. It was strange how he felt immediately comfortable in her presence. The smell and feel of her were strangely familiar, but such was the noise from the spa orchestra that conversation was impossible.

At a break they stole out onto the balcony and shivered in the harsh sea breeze but were excited by the crashing whiteness of the waves. Out of such controlled warmth and civilisation they had now entered a world of manic nature and random beauty. Then came an even greater shock for Sidney as the girl eased off her cat mask.

"It's you, isn't it, Sidney?"

"Popsy?"

"I knew we would meet again. It's good to see you."

"And I you."

"Are you still…"

"Living at River View? Yes, I am, but the plan is to move before the winter arrives."

And although that was not the truth, the situation earlier with the devil mask had enabled him to share Popsy's personal sense of fear with River View. So now it was clear that he would choose his marriage over his house and River View would be once more up for auction and subject to further speculation about the omens that surrounded it.

Within the week, Sidney Yedman had packed and gone to live at Filey and informed the auctioneer from whom he had bought the house that it was to be put out again to tender.

And yet it was not quite the end of his association with me. He was to return at a later date and in a different capacity.

*

CHAPTER SIX: *The Grocer's Tale*

Time passed and no buyer could be found. On three separate occasions, Sidney Yedman agreed to drop his asking price. Yet still no one stepped forward. Freeman and Farrow called Sidney in and said that it was a difficult time and there was no prospect of a sale without he drastically reduced his reserve. Reluctantly, for he had put much work and material into the cottage, he consented.

The sale, when it occurred, was not by auction and the purchaser was a local man: one Frederick Archer, a grocer by trade. He had espied River View Cottage many months earlier, but waited until the time was right. The instant the price reduction was declared, he made a bold bid and said he would wait but one calendar month.

He prided himself on having bought a bargain and gave no credence whatsoever to darkly muttered stories about cursed cottages. Such embroidered tales were mere tittle tattle. To him life was about transaction and good judgement, material acquisition and subsequent well-being. Matters of the spirit, whether they were prayers to an imagined God or stories told on the premise that the dead had returned, were best consigned to oblivion.

That he had acquired 'a chocolate box cottage' at such a bargain price transcended all other considerations. It was an achievement that underlined the twin virtues of patience and perspicacity.

He was on the surface an intensely cheerful man with a wife of fickle health and a son who rarely attended school.

This son, Norman, was over-indulged by the wife and mother, one Margaret Archer. She implanted in Norman's mind the idea that he was a sickly child and that schools were dangerous places where disease was rife.

Unprepossessing in appearance, Archer was a slightly built man with a beard that was turning white before he entered his forties. His narrowed eyes seemed to be permanently squinting at a non-existent sun and reinforced the perception that he was always in the business of contemplating how to make the best of difficult circumstances. Yet he was not miserable, nor so tightly focused that others thought him narrow-minded or self-obsessed. He could dip in his pocket to buy acquaintances a drink and always laughed generously at another's jokes.

He looked now at his partner, Margaret. She lacked his social graces and had a limited focus. She overdressed on a daily basis, hats and scarves in abundance, carrying winter's attitudes into the height of summer. Most of all, she imprinted her obsessions on their son, a sickly-looking pale lad who hid behind outsize spectacles. It was he she spoke about now.

"Consumption is everywhere, Frederick. It is better I keep the boy at home. We cannot take the risk of losing our only child. I will educate him for the next term until it is safe to return."

Archer knew this to be a gross exaggeration on two accounts: consumption was dying out nationally and his wife, a woman without culture, was incapable of giving the boy anything but a rudimentary education.

Archer worked hard to earn a good living for his small family in whom he was deeply disappointed. He had a wife with whom sexual fulfilment seemed as unlikely as was realising the hope that his son would develop into a worthwhile heir.

He could not understand why his wife did not show more gratitude at living in such an idyllic rural retreat. It was the house of Frederick's dreams, (since childhood he had dreamed of living in a house with a stream at the bottom of the garden) and he could not understand why Margaret found it ordinary at best, threatening at worst.

"This is a house of character, Margaret. Some people would give their right hand for a house in the country like this, with a river running by. We are blessed if only you could appreciate it."

"Me - I'd rather live in the town in something modern," she told him, "Traffic running past, the sounds of people leading their busy lives. Hmmphh, you can keep your rivers and trees and fields."

For dramatic effect Archer froze like a statue in the middle of the room. He raised an index finger to his lips.

"Stop what you're doing, Margaret. Listen. This house has atmosphere, it has a voice."

They paused. The only 'voice' Margaret could hear was the roar of the swollen river racing beyond the window after heavy overnight rain.

"That doesn't reassure me, Freddie. I find the idea of a talking house scary."

"Oh use your imagination, woman. What a marvellous building it will be for young Norman to grow up in. History and character."

In the weeks that followed many were the times that Archer, determined to make a success of his new business at his expanding store in Scarborough town, would return home in the late evening to find his son tucked up in bed and his wife sprawled out on the settee. She would be half-listening to the radio and any meal she had cooked for him would be reduced to a desiccated disaster as a result of long hours spent in the warming oven.

By now the trappings of human anger were as familiar to me as the wretched silence that filled my rooms on the many occasions that I was uninhabited. Frederick Archer was a ticking time bomb. One evening, when he was especially late home, he saw no point in returning to an indigestible meal and opted instead for the comforts of the Cock and Feathers. It was in there that the landlord, Gordon Hamshaw, recounted to Archer what he knew of the bizarre history of the house he lived in. Being a relative of the original Hamshaw, he was able to give full details going back almost a century. Archer was at once fascinated, unconvinced and repulsed.

"We have lived there six months, landlord," he said, "and I have seen nor heard anything untoward."

"What about the casement windows?" Hamshaw teased.

"What about 'em? Very neat little things, if you ask me. Old railway stock. They're what first drew me to the house," Archer replied.

“Miss Groves, who often popped in here for a snifter,” the landlord said, “always told us there was something about those smaller windows. Something not to be trusted.”

“Not to be trusted? What could she have meant?”

“Don’t ask me,” Hamshaw said, with mock innocence, “I couldn’t pin her down. She just muttered something about atmosphere…”

“Fascinating!” Archer said, “I must have a word with her sometime.”

“You’d have a job,” Hamshaw said, and told the tale of how she had met her fate at the end of a rope in the outside lavatory of River View Cottage. Archer had to listen with rapt attention for Hamshaw had something of a speech impediment and his voice travelled from a point deep down in his throat. This had the effect of drawing the listener deeper into the conversation than perhaps he intended.

Now although Archer had put on an act of being unmoved by what he had heard up to this point, the fact that a poor soul had recently chosen her own death within his outhouse undoubtedly did disturb him. He went very quiet and asked the landlord for a double whisky.

I have heard it said by my inhabitants that ‘fate works in strange ways’ and at that point Jacob Browne, a Cock and Feathers regular, entered the premises for his nightly jar of ale. He took his regular seat on a bar stool, opposite Hamshaw.

“Has Gracie pupped yet?” the landlord asked him, saying to anyone who would listen, “Jacob has a Jack Russell due to give birth any time.”

"Gracie had four pups last week," Browne said in maudlin tones, "but by the time a couple of days had passed only two had survived."

"And what are you planning to do with them?" the landlord enquired.

"Why, I shall keep one for myself and probably drown the other," Browne replied tersely.

Archer's ears perked up. This was a heaven sent opportunity to get young Norman active and to inject a little life into that mausoleum of a house.

"I'll take the pup off you, Mr Browne," Archer interrupted, "I'll even buy you a drink on the strength of it."

The bargain was struck and by midnight Archer was accompanying Browne to his modest cottage on the outskirts of the village to collect the puppy. There the two men had a further drink before Archer, pup under his arm, returned home.

My walls have been witness to many men whose judgment has been warped by drink. Using his own key to enter the house, Archer found progress suddenly barred to him; the door was bolted from the inside.

Setting the pup on the step, Archer proceeded to hammer furiously on the door. As one minute developed into ten, the braying on the door became so ferocious that my walls vibrated with the friction. Eventually, an uninviting Margaret Archer, wrapped in thick dressing gown, scarf and hat, opened the door:

"What are you doing, man? We're all asleep in here. It's almost tomorrow."

At that point Archer snapped. Grabbing his wife by the collar of her nightdress with one hand and her fleshy elbow by the other, he dragged her down the garden path. She screamed in such abject terror that cottage dwellers on the other side of the water turned on their lights in concert.

"No, no, don't do this," Archer's wife begged as he manoeuvred her closer and closer to the river.

"I cannot swim, Frederick. Please stop now."

There was a loud splash as her pneumatic form was dumped off the bank.

"I cannot swim, I cannot swim," she shouted nonstop.

But Archer was not listening. He was back within my walls and striding upstairs, terrified puppy under his arm, barging into his son's bedroom with a fury that caused the door to bang against the wall.

"There! I got this for you, Norman," he said, dropping the young dog on his son's blanketed form, "do something with it."

He responded in the manner his mother had taught him. He blubbered like there was no tomorrow. His crying found an echo from the prostrate figure of his mother on the front steps, seated in a puddle of her own making. Fortunately the river had only been waist-high so once her balance was recovered Margaret Archer had crawled onto the bank and, like some primeval amphibian, dragged herself up to the door that was now locked against *her.*

Still drunk, Archer told his wife through the closed front door to go and jump back in the river when she demanded that he open up to her. But such had been his exertions that Archer then collapsed onto the Chesterfield and drifted into an alcoholic haze. Eventually it was young Norman who crept downstairs to open the door to his distressed mother.

Once Margaret Archer could see that Frederick was so far gone as to be unreachable, she stopped her tears and dragged Norman up to the bedroom where she packed bags for both of them. The puppy cringed in a corner of the bedroom, totally fazed by the many events it had experienced in the last 24 hours.

For the second time within my keeping, a family had been rent asunder. I knew how the village people would react to this: they would say it was the curse of my four walls. I could hear it now: ‘No relationship can survive within that cursed building.’

“What will we do, mother? Where will we go? What of father?” young Norman quizzed.

“We’ll find a lodging place in the town, Norman.”

“Will we live near to the sea?” asked Norman, keen to take make the most of a misfortune.

“Is that what you want?”

“Living near the sea will be so much better than the river, mother.”

“Then you shall be near the sea, Norman.”

“And my father?”

“He is a drunken sot and will wake to his own company.”

“But he brought me a puppy dog. I should like to keep it.”

“That’s not possible, Norman. Lodgers cannot bring animals with them.”

"Then I'll cry," Norman declared, promptly fulfilling his promise.

"If you keep crying, then I shall leave you here with your puppy and your drunken father," his mother said, proving that she could use discipline when it suited her.

With that she grabbed a bag in each hand and, with a toss of her head, indicated the direction in which Norman should propel himself. How she progressed from there to the town at such an ungodly hour, heaven knows, but generally I observe that people find a will where one is called for.

Archer was in a bad state when he awoke; a condition that was made worse by a warm faecal aroma.

"Margaret, Norman. Which of us has shit the bed?" he slurred.

Archer's upper body hurt him where he had been pulling and twisting the substantial weight of Margaret while fuelled by drink. The dog – which he had forgotten about - cowered in the corner of the bedroom; mortified at standing in its own waste and terrified by the house's atmosphere.

Archer's feelings were ambivalent. He was deeply ashamed of his part in the previous night's shenanigans, but not sorry at the departure of his wife and son. On inspection of the house, the signs were that this was no casual flit.

"Well, so be it," he said aloud. "Let them beg to be readmitted when they have thought about things and drummed up the courage."

Next he must take a decision about the dog. His original reason for bringing it to the house had disappeared and might not return, but there was now the prospect of his own aloneness. He decided on those grounds alone he would keep the dog for the time being and so lifted it into the sink and scrubbed it clean.

"I shall call you Lincoln," he said to it, "because that is where I am headed on business today. First, young pup, I'll get you some food in the village."

This choice of name for his new found canine companion was inexplicable. We houses, comprised as we are of earth, stone, metal and wood, do not recognise such things as coincidences. There is always an underlying reason for the way things happen.

Margaret and her son Norman Archer eventually acquired their own terraced house for a rent in nearby Scarborough. She wrote her husband a note, explaining that for the sum of £20 a month, she was happy to preserve the status quo and no questions asked. Frederick made one half-hearted, doomed attempt to ask forgiveness, visiting the address with a sad posy of flowers.

It was not difficult for Frederick to meet Margaret's financial demands. His grocery business in the town of Scarborough was thriving to the point where he had opened a second shop in the town of Pickering some 12 miles to the west. He gabbled to himself incessantly as he paced within my walls, talking of his plans for the future and how he would channel his energy into work and business success now that a family life was to be denied him.

Put it down to the fact that Frederick had now become self-absorbed that he seemed unworried by living in a house of ill-repute and fearful legends. His entire consciousness was preoccupied with thoughts of commercial success. However, it occurred to him one night, quite out of the blue, that Lincoln hardly ever seemed to spend time in the living room. The dog went upstairs at night as company for him and was fed in the kitchen. But during the day the sun rotated round the front of the house pouring light into the south-facing living room window. Surely, it was only natural for a dog to luxuriate in the sun's warmth. Yet whenever Archer returned from work, he was aware that Lincoln always bounded down the stairs to greet him, never from the one room in the house to benefit from the sun's radiance.

This phenomenon made Archer curious and he decided to investigate it. Picking up the Jack Russell from its resting place on the landing rug, he carried it downstairs.

At first the dog was not duly concerned. When Archer was at home in an evening, the dog often accompanied him in the living room, but never went near the smaller casement windows. Archer had noticed that. The dog even threw occasional furtive glances in that direction.

"This is silly, Lincoln. It's only a building. Is there something in the corner over there? A rat or mouse perhaps? Some vermin? Well, then earn your corn and see it off."

With that, Archer picked up the unfortunate terrier and carried it to that corner of the room immediately beneath one of the casement windows.

If Archer undertook the task lightly, then he soon regretted it. The dog, normally mild-mannered and given to a comic turn, transformed into an electric bundle of terror that Archer could no longer hold in his arms. Its hackles rose vertically and its lips peeled back revealing a countenance associated more with a hell-hound. Sheer fear that he might sustain a rabid bite made Archer drop the dog immediately and retreat to the kitchen doorway. Too late he realised that he was blocking the dog's escape route once it had opted for flight rather than fight. On the way past him, it snapped at and tore a snip of his trouser leg, an act utterly out of character.

Feeling sorrow rather than anger for the demented beast, from then on he took it daily into work with him. Rather than leaving it alone in the house when he got home, Archer let it accompany him on his nightly trip to the Cock and Feathers. There he chanced to tell the landlord, Gordon Hamshaw, what had just happened.

"With due respects, Mr Archer, sir," (everyone in the locality knew that Archer had gone up in the world and was to be respected), "I did tell you what that Miss Groves used to say about the casement windows in your dwelling," Hamshaw reminded him.

"Just go over that story once again, landlord," Archer asked him.

"Well, it aren't much of a story, sir. She allus said she had unpleasant feelings about them windows. She could never figure it out because she said it was always told to her that River View, River Cottage as you have called it now, was an old railway house and what was to mistrust about a railway house."

For a second or two, Archer looked mystified at Hamshaw's observation. Then the penny dropped.

"Oh yes. She took her own life in the air raid shelter, didn't she?"

"Which used to be the outside netty, Mr Archer," Hamshaw said with a grin.

Archer went home to think on the story Hamshaw had told him. He paused at his own gate and pondered yet again upon the relatively young oak tree in the lawn border. Was it one oak tree twisted or was it two oak trees growing from the same foundation? Maybe it was simply a freak of nature. In the end he had to accept he was ignorant of anything to do with the soil.

Of course, he could not see the small boy lying there, four feet down in the soil, roots of oak growing from the bony remnants of his hands. It was a fact which no living person could reveal as the boy had been buried long ago by Binns and his wife in the gypsy tradition at the dead of night.

Archer had grown unexpectedly fond of his little dog and was reluctant to subject it to anymore time alone at River Cottage. Back home he snuggled down in bed, then patted the blanket, inviting Lincoln to join him.

Propped up on a pillow, stroking the dog, he made a pronouncement to the pampered creature. I took in every word he said.

"You and I, Lincoln – we will move to Pickering. We shall live above my shop and make that our home. I shall appoint a manager at the Scarborough shop and work there each Monday and Saturday. River Cottage and all its so-called ghosts will become a holiday home. It is not for us, little dog. We move out the house tomorrow."

With that, he turned off the light and man and dog went to sleep. I could do nothing but accept in silence what my new fate was to be.

Within four weeks, Archer had workmen in at both addresses; converting River Cottage to holiday accommodation and upstairs at his grocery shop in Pickering to a live-in flat. I acquired proper guttering and down pipes. My upstairs window frames were renewed and the roof re-tiled. Inside, the decorators mounted wallpaper where none had been and applied new paint to make my interior almost unrecognisable. A phone line was installed.

Archer was a pure businessman and no aesthete. As far as things of beauty were concerned he would proudly announce to anyone who would listen that he knew what he liked even if he couldn't tell them why he liked it: music, paintings, the world around him; it applied to them all.

That judgment applied to River View Cottage, but not to the laburnum that annually blossomed in the tiny front garden. He loved that time of year. Often he would lie in bed of a morning, the curtains drawn back just so he could admire the brilliant golden flowers that dripped from the branches of the tree like frozen teardrops.

One of the workmen he had employed as a painter approached him with bad news.

"Do you know anything about trees, Mr Archer?"

He told him he had not the slightest knowledge.

"Well, I do and I think you're about to lose that laburnum in front of your lawn."

"It's dying?"

"Aye, it is. The curious thing about it though is that only half of its dying. Look!"

And he pointed out that one half of the tree was budding perfectly, but the half nearest the river had gone barren. It would bear no flowers. And the trunk of the tree was badly scarred, as though someone had been stabbing it with a knife.

"Is there anything I can do to rescue it?" he asked the man.

"No, it will die completely, but it might take a year or two."

"Is it dangerous? Should I get it chopped down?"

"Up to you."

More trouble, thought Archer. But he pushed the matter of the tree to the back of his mind. After all, hadn't the painter told him it was good for a few years yet?

Friends he had cultivated at the Round Table advised him of a fair rent for a holiday let; Archer exceeded their figure by 20 per cent and promptly placed it with an agent who block-booked it for the summer.

It was not as distressing as those long weeks and months when no one dwelled within my walls, but now people moved through my spaces in snapshots rather than experiencing me as part of the film of their lives.

To most of my short stay occupants, I was unremarkable. Occasionally, children would say things to their parents like 'Mummy, I don't like it here.' Once a small girl asked her mother where the bloodstain on the floor had come from. Puzzled, her mother asked her "What mark is that, darling?"

The girl pointed to the floor where Ashcroft had been slain by Lincoln; but I had long since been scrubbed clean and the adult saw only a slate surface.

Some holiday-makers even sat by the casement windows, but this was largely the prerogative of the old. They would sit there for a middle-of-the-day snooze or to read a book. Most of them would finish up looking over their shoulders, feeling inexplicably uncomfortable and moving away.

Time and again, I would hear people announce in their ignorance that this must have been an old railway house.

"How do you know that, Terry?" one weekender asked her husband.

"You can tell by the livery. Look at those railings and the decorative woodwork… and I noticed the remains of an old train line just down the road."

"But how could a railway come through here – there are trees everywhere?"

"They've been planted quite recently. Within the last 40 years."

To many visitors, their discomfort in River Cottage manifested itself in unremarkable ways: a poor night's sleep; constant fidgeting and the inability to sit down; uneasiness at being left alone in a room; being disturbed and afraid because of my constant shifts and cracks

Then came Carmel Ferguson.

*

CHAPTER SEVEN: *The Spiritualist's Tale*

"Nice little ex-railway cottage we're stopping in this time," I heard a man's voice proclaim from just outside the front door.

He was Robert Ferguson: an eccentric musician with a strange gait, (his progress was a waddle rather than a walk), an inclination to always dress formally and an annoying habit of rubbing the back of his hand across his lips.

The woman who accompanied him stood stock still outside the front gate staring at the oak tree. She had gone deathly silent.

"What's the problem, Carmel?" her husband asked. "It's just an oak tree."

"No, it's not" she told him, with no room for argument, "it's two oak trees and beneath them is the tragic end of a life."

For most people such a statement would have been alarming, for the shockproof Robert Ferguson it was the kind of insight that issued often from his wife's lips.

From the moment he first crossed my threshold I could see that he was a man in awe of his wife and at first I could not see why. She was neither loud nor domineering; hers was a quiet assured presence.

Her husband led her into the house, relieved to put down the suitcases and crack his knuckles. Immediately behind him, his wife Carmel stopped dead the moment she set foot inside the door and looked up at the ceiling.

“Oh my goodness,” she uttered, as though the décor of the room was a shock to the system or a spectral presence had greeted them once inside the building.

“What now, Carmel?” He said this not in a bored or long-suffering way, but in a respectful tone that showed Carmel had a long history of such warnings.

“Robert, you must be able to feel it, even a pachyderm like you.”

‘Pachyderm’, it was one of her favourite terms when highlighting her partner’s lack of psychic awareness. Ferguson knew exactly what she was saying. He had jousted with his wife over her ‘unique powers’ for many a year. Any doubts he had about their existence had long ago been dispelled by actual events.

She stood almost a foot taller than Robert. Although in her early fifties, she looked much younger. Not a trace yet of grey in her hair. Her features were larger than average for a woman, but perfectly proportioned with a soft satiny complexion. The striking thing about Carmel was her voice. It spoke with resonance and control. It held her listeners, whoever they might be. It held her husband now.

“What is it I’m supposed to be able to feel?”

“Nothing you can see. Plenty you can sense; a smell even.”

She was a formidable woman. I recognised that much. Whatever she could feel about me, I reciprocated. There was an electric atmosphere about the lady and I knew she must be treated with respect.

“Tobacco smoke, you mean?” Robert replied, sniffing the air and being intentionally banal, “maybe there was a family of smokers before us, so what? The smell of tobacco clings to a place, Carmel. Filthy habit."

"Stop belittling me like that, Robert. I don't mean something as nondescript as tobacco smoke. The entire house is full of broken spirits. This room alone has been the scene of more tragedies than I can count. People have died in here, and not so very long ago. And…oh, oh, oh…"

Suddenly his wife, normally a calm person, was on the edge of hysteria. Robert Ferguson, no stranger to the effects of her psychic talents, realised this was no overreaction.

"What is it, Carmel, what is it? Come and sit down."

"The windows, the windows. Over there," she said, pointing at the small casement windows. Of all the people who had entered my premises, I had never seen such an acute reaction. She knew. In the very fibre of her being she knew. Before her, my past was laid bare.

Ferguson looked where she pointed, but could see nothing. So perturbed was his wife that he had to help her out of the house, into the front garden and the fresh air.

"Carmel, I've never seen you like this before. You're so disturbed. Why? It must be bad. What is it?"

"I've never been in a house like this one before. I tell you it is full of the dead and…" at this point she struggled to say more. Robert stared at her with a paralysis in his look. He could not move on until she completed her sentence.

"And what, Carmel? What else apart from the dead? What could be worse than the dead?"

"The undead, Robert," she said. "The undead are here too."

Of course he did not know what she meant. Why, surely the undead were none other than themselves, the living. How else could one interpret that description? Ferguson could not see beyond that.

His wife was not about to explain either. Something had to be done. Then she steadied herself. Her demeanour became more business-like. It was as though with a snap of the metaphorical fingers she returned to the here and now.

"Robert, I want you to contact the landlord and get him over here."

Ferguson grimaced at the authoritarian tone of his wife's demand, seeing only a difficult situation for himself. Yet he knew she meant it and there would be good reason for it and argument would not be brooked.

"If I must" he said with heavy heart.

"You really must," she answered.

Archer had installed a house phone. Next to it was a notebook for logging calls. On its cover was a simple message – 'We trust your honesty'.

Carmel nodded and struggled, breathing like an asthmatic although she wasn't one.

She stood in the living room while Robert made the phone call, inhaling with effort the air around the casement windows. She cut a detective-like figure, one trying to solve a murder mystery.

Archer was shocked and inconvenienced by Robert Ferguson's call. So much information in such a tiny snatch of time. He told him there was no chance he could come over before lunch. The shop was busy and he had accounts to attend to. Business must take precedent.

"Mr Archer, my wife asked me to call you urgently. She says there are things you need to know about your house. My wife has special powers and I tell you no lie. When she says that something is wrong, I always listen. You may or may not believe in those powers, Mr Archer, but I have never known her to be wrong about these things."

It went silent on the other end of the line for a full minute.

"Are you still there, Mr Archer?"

The message went against every grain of common sense Archer possessed. And yet there was something insistent about the man's tone. It would be foolish to ignore it.

"I'm thinking over what you said. I need to contact the girl who does part-time for me. It'll take a while."

In the end, it was agreed that Archer would come by mid-afternoon. Ferguson returned to his wife.

"He says he'll be here by three."

Carmel's expression was pained. "We cannot stay here a moment longer on our own."

Ferguson thought better than to argue. The pair of them decided to repair to the Cock and Feathers rather than remain in the holiday home.

Gordon Hamshaw, the barman, was struck by the woman's appearance the second she set foot in the lounge.

"Are you all right, love? Look a bit pasty," he observed as the Fergusons asked for a couple of strong coffees at the bar.

"She's had a bit of a fright. We're staying at the holiday cottage – River View or whatever it's called," Ferguson told him in a strong Birmingham accent.

"Not from round here then?"

While Carmel slumped at a corner table, Ferguson explained that they were staying in the holiday cottage next the river.

"It has a bit of a history does that old cottage," Hamshaw said in loud tones, "It's an old cottage belonging to the railway."

"Why do you call it a railway cottage?" Carmel asked, cutting into the conversation from across the room, a sharpness in her voice.

"People round here have always called it that," the landlord said, "I suppose it's because it's set near the old railway line and it has white railings. Looks like a stationmaster's cottage.

"Well, it's not one," Carmel informed him, "That house used to be a church."

At that, Hamshaw burst out laughing. "You what, missus? I've lived round these parts all my life and there's never been a church there. I'm pretty sure there weren't in my grandparents' day neither."

"There wasn't," Carmel rapped back, "the church was brought to the place. That house is constructed from an old church."

That was said with such conviction it stopped the landlord in his tracks. "No, it can't be. How can you move a whole church? In any case, how would you know that, lady?"

Ferguson chipped in. "Don't ask her that, mister. She never knows how she knows, but honestly, she knows. She has a gift"

Suddenly there descended a frostiness in the Cock and Feathers air. There were just four locals present in the bar and they openly chided the Fergusons for this new revelation. Locals hate to be told that knowledge learned at the knee is incorrect at the best of times; to be told by an 'incomer' is nothing less than insulting.

For her part, when her powers were at their strongest, Carmel Ferguson had no place for tact or diplomacy.

"I tell you what I know to be the truth and that is unalterable," she said, "what do I care whether or not you believe me?"

The Fergusons left the pub after an uncomfortable sandwich lunch spent largely in a silence that permeated the entire lounge. Gordon Hamshaw flashed the V sign at their backs as they exited the lounge, much to the laughter and approval of the few locals.

Over the years, a turning circle and small parking area had been established at the weir of the river next to Archer's property. First the advent of the motor car and then Archer's business acumen had played no small part in this development.

"Hello, Mr and Mrs Ferguson," said Archer, who was waiting for them as they returned to River Cottage for their three'o'clock meeting. Archer wore his standard 'Hail fellow well met' countenance; all part of the successful businessman. His overstated smile was not returned by the Fergusons.

"Now what can I do for you good people? I trust there's nothing wrong with the accommodation, I haven't had a single complaint all year."

"Oh, but there is, Mr Archer," Carmel responded, "there is something very wrong," whereupon Archer's smile slipped down to his feet. He could see that Carmel Ferguson was not a woman to be argued with.

"Oh, I'm sorry to hear that," Archer said. "The important thing is what can we do about it?"

But Carmel ignored this and took control. "Mr Archer, what do you know about this cottage you own? Have you lived in it yourself?"

"Yes, I have lived in it. At one point my entire family lived in it. I know that many years ago it was a railway cottage. Where is this taking us, Mrs Ferguson?"

She paused and gave Archer a lingering stare. She turned and pointed to the twisted oak tree. "Do you know anything about why that tree is like that?"

Archer smiled warmly. "No, nothing; strange, isn't it?" he said with an affected nonchalance.

"It's like that because there is a dead child beneath it," Carmel informed him casually.

Neither he nor Robert Ferguson one could follow that revelation. Archer scratched his head and waited for Carmel to continue.

If he was waiting for some significant pronouncement he was to be disappointed. All she said was "Will you follow me inside?"

Once inside, she requested that all three of them sit at a small table which she had placed by the casement windows. She ignored all of Archer's protestations that he must be back in town by close of business. In truth they were token resistance; it was abundantly clear that his curiosity was getting the better of him.

"Mr Archer, I do not believe this is a railway cottage at all," she said. "I know this house to have been built from a church…"

"How can you know that? How can you know that?" Archer rattled out, "You don't come from these parts…"

Ferguson did not know for certain that I was originally built from a church but he was ready to take up the cudgels for his wife.. There was no written evidence, but testimony to his wife's powers of perception had been uttered by hundreds of people in countless places and occasions down the years.

Robert Ferguson replied with that same softly spoken confidence. "Mr Archer, my wife has a gift. She is never wrong about these things. If she says this was a church, then that will be the truth of the matter."

Archer said nothing, but stared at Carmel with something close to hostility. Carmel, for her part, ignored the implied aggression and pointed to the casement windows.

"What do you know about those windows, Mr Archer? Even you can see that they are not in the proper style of a railway house."

Archer remembered the startling reaction of his dog Lincoln to being left in this room, close to these windows. He knew that was the reason he had taken the dog to new quarters. Conversely, there was little room in his life for uncomfortable truths. This was a problem better ignored.

"They are casement windows and I dare say the builder put them there as an add-on when the rest had been built."

"Mr Archer, they are no 'add-on'. Those window frames date back hundreds of years. Yes, maybe the glass is more recent," Carmel told him, "but those windows were part of the church that made up this building. I know enough about architecture to say that."

Archer felt belittled and uncomfortable in his own holiday cottage. He felt hot under the collar and was tired from wrestling with the end of year accounts and being pestered by Mrs Archer for an increase in his agreed alimony sum.

"So the windows may be old as the hills; what is it you want me to do?"

Ferguson took up the thread for his wife. Over the years he had grown used to the disparagement of those who thought Carmel's powers were a cheap trick. He was beyond being astonished by her inexplicable perceptions. All he knew was that when she was as certain as she now appeared to be she was never wrong. Sometimes her sense of the past lacked conviction and on those occasions he said very little, just waiting for Carmel to know or move on because the signal was weak. This time she was sure.

There was no room for doubt in the way he now spoke to Archer. She had briefed him on the way back from the Cock and Feathers about what needed to be done. Seconds earlier she had tipped him the nod across the room indicating that now was the time.

"Carmel wants us to sit round a table in this room, holding hands. She feels that this is the important room in the house. If the living hold hands and become as one, then the departed will feel able to speak through her."

"The departed – who are they? And does that mean we are the living?" said Archer, with more than a trace of sarcasm in his voice, but also finally needled at being ordered around in his own property as well as the prospect of holding hands with two strangers.

But he was mesmerised by events and kept his counsel as Ferguson prepared the seats round the table beneath the casement windows. With a speed of movement that defied description, Carmel grabbed hold of the hands of both men and commenced a deep groaning sound that Archer found profoundly disturbing. Yet he dare not let go; so shocked was he by the speed of events.

She looked up to the ceiling; sheer terror registering on her new made face. Her voice, when it came out was unmistakeably a man's voice, "Fenby, Fenby," it screamed, "for God's sake, take it off him."

After an internal wrestle that lasted fully a minute, she let go of both men's hands and fell to the floor, groaning and clutching the top of her head. Archer got up from his chair and started forward in a bid to assist Carmel off the floor.

"Don't do that, Mr Archer," Ferguson said, restraining the landlord by blocking his path. She lay for some time on that same spot on the floor in a state of perfect stillness. To all appearances life had ceased to flow through her. Archer thought the entire business was extremely bizarre although at no point did he think he was being 'taken for a ride'.

These people believed in what they were doing. Of that he was sure.

Just when it seemed she would lay there for eternity, there was a slight movement; her lips opened and shut resembling a fish's breathing. Moving with deliberation she sat upright and spoke:

"Richard was cursed by what you did," she said, though no one present had any idea who she addressed, nor were it came from. Of course I knew. I knew that she was slipping in and out of the ghostly personalities that were trapped within my walls. She had been Ashcroft and had now transformed into Amelia Binns. They were near perfect echoes.

She appeared to 'come to' and, slowly, but with dignity, climbed back into her chair and this time placed her hands over her eyes. I knew what was happening. She had become a part of me, herself a part of the house. It was as though she was at once inside the very walls and a part of them.

I had never met a person with such powers. We were as one, Carmel and I. There was no past time with her now. All time was of one dimension: the point at which the two forces met.

Archer was humbled, now convinced that he was dealing with a power beyond his imagination. In a croaky voice, he was afraid to address Carmel directly, only through her husband.

"The windows!" Archer barked, "Earlier she said something about the windows. Please ask her about them. Can you do that? I want to know about the windows."

Ignoring him, Ferguson knelt forward so as to make no noise. “Carmel, who are you now?”

She sat up tight and looked directly at the casement window. Resuming a man’s voice, she spoke “Ashcroft. I am still Ashcroft. Fenby did not protect me.”

“So what happened?”

“Lincoln killed me. Oh, the blood,” she said and with an index finger traced an imaginary flow of blood down her face.

Tension took hold of Archer at the mention of the name Lincoln. Lincoln was his dog, but she could not have known that.

(Of course, the dog’s naming was mere coincidence, if you believe in such things. After all, Archer had no awareness of the man who had been architect of this building, but maybe a fleeting resonance of the man’s existence had darted into his head and suggested the dog’s name. But the reason he had settled on the dog’s name, he recalled, was a business trip to that city).

“Please ask your wife, Mrs Ferguson, about the windows.”

Ferguson looked at him with incomprehension and then turned towards his wife.

“Ashcroft, do you know about the windows? Can you tell us about the windows?”

Where Ferguson was unmoved when his wife spoke as a man, Archer jumped with shock. He had never before witnessed a female exhibiting such a powerful male aura. She not only sounded like a man but her male aura could be sensed in the atmosphere.

"Oh they are fine, fine windows. I told the boys to carry them with care."

"Where? Where did they carry them from?" Ferguson asked her.

"They were part of St Mary's church, in the Forge Valley. The best part. Beautiful, don't you think?"

"They are fine windows, Ashcroft. What makes them special?"

And now the most incredible occurrence.

Carmel began to shape-change at an alarming rate. Archer could only watch in astonishment. Her body seemed to have another presence within that was pushing at the flesh in different places. Even the skull distorted at times. She stood up, she sat down. She lay on the floor and rolled over like two people fighting. Archer was alarmed and began to intervene. The anger on Ferguson's face made him freeze.

There was calm and Carmel returned to her seat. Her posture and demeanour changed yet again. She was in control now, barely breathing but basking in a kind of majesty.

Archer dare not even look at the woman. After a lengthy silence, Ferguson spoke.

"Who are you now?" he demanded.

"I am the reverend."

"The reverend who?" Ferguson questioned relentlessly.

"The Reverend of St Mary's, the Reverend Godfrey Merryweather."

"What year is it, Reverend Merryweather?"

"Sixteen sixty-eight.

“I want to know about the windows, Godfrey.”

“I am sorry, who are you? A villager. A commoner. To you, I am the Reverend Merryweather. Please address me that way. Only in God’s eyes am I Godfrey.”

But Ferguson pressed on. “Mr Archer and I wondered about the windows of your church, the casement windows.”

“Ah, it’s a shame we must use them in such a way, but at least I do my best to ensure that those within, the dead and dying, are safe from the devil. A candle burns…always.”

“How do the windows serve you, Reverend?”

“They allow light in the side room where the dead are held. No crypt was ever dug out for this church. It was a foolish oversight.”

“Where the dead are held? Why are the bodies being held there? Why do you not bury them?”

“Because they are dying faster than I can bury them. I am consoler of the dying, grave-digger and minister at funerals. I am also the only one who can keep the candle burning. So many tasks for just one man.”

“Sixteen sixty-eight, it is a plague year, yes?”

“It is indeed. Brought to us by a traveller from Paris.”

“There is much fear in the community?”

“Indeed, there is. The greatest fear is that we bury the living among the dead. I am many things, but not a physician. Sometimes I cannot confidently discern the living from the dead. A heartbeat can be so faint as to be undetectable.

“And yet the corpses of the dead must be removed from the lives of the living lest they infect them.”

“Are you the only one who can do this?” Ferguson asked his wife acting in the persona of Godfrey Merryweather.

“Mistakes are inevitable. One man can do only so much. I am many things to many people. I am many things…I am… I am the Reverend Godfrey Merry…”

And with this fading speech Carmel Ferguson stuttered to a halt. She sat bolt upright in her chair, neither moving nor speaking. She stayed like that for what seemed an age.

No one moved. Ferguson was almost as statuesque as his wife. Archer was petrified by events too – a stranger within his own property.

After time had passed, taking care not to disturb Carmel, Ferguson crossed the room to the small side table on which the phone rested.

“I need to use your phone” he told Archer without pausing.

In hurried tones, he called a taxi. Archer said not a word during Ferguson’s phone call. He remained transfixed by the woman who had just astounded him with her powers. This scenario was a far cry from anything he had envisaged when he got up that morning to start his day.

“You are not staying here?” he asked when Ferguson had completed his call.

“I don’t think that would be wise now. I need to get Carmel away. If it’s the money that concerns you -

“No, no. Of course not. You must do what you think is best.”

The pair sat in silence awaiting the arrival of the taxi.

“Shouldn’t you bring her round, wake her up?” Archer asked once Ferguson had ended the phone call.

“Oh no. The spirits will leave her body in their own time and Carmel will return,” Ferguson said, “to do otherwise will endanger Carmel.”

“May we talk?” Archer asked, “Will it disturb her?”

Ferguson nodded. It was a tacit assent. Archer continued.

“So she – your wife - became another person?”

“She became two, three, four people, Mr Archer. Multiple personalities, it is called. She is well capable of that.”

“I thought she told us, as the vicar, that the casement windows guarded a section of the church where those dead and dying from the plague were laid out? Is that what she told us?”

“Yes. This building before it was a house was a church without a crypt. It was the Reverend Godfrey Merryweather who told us, Mr Archer. That was who Carmel had become.”

These men could only speculate how hundreds of years had passed since the horrors of 1668 but my fabric still echoed with the horror of what had happened.

The dying were laid amongst the dead and there they moaned all night long and into the following day. Constantly the plague-ridden turned to their neighbours for help, only to be confronted by a desperate rictus, a grim cadaver that was beyond help or giving help. Is it possible to imagine the horror of that?

During that time the only sources of illumination were the moonlight when it pierced the heavy foliage outside the church and penetrated those casement windows and the few candles that Merryweather could be bothered to light.

Archer stood up and looked about the house as if he was seeing it anew. For once that part of him he called his business brain was bypassed. He was cooling towards the idea of River View Cottage as part of a portfolio.

Suddenly he broke the silence with a dramatic declamation.

"I'm not sure that I can keep this on as a holiday property. There is too much past contained within its walls."

Ferguson had by now eased his wife into a lounge chair. Her eyelids flickered but she was not yet fully conscious.

"Your wife – is she all right? Should I call a doctor?" Archer asked.

"I've seen this before – many times," Ferguson said, "it might take her an hour or so to come round, but she'll be okay."

"And when she does, will she be able to remember what she went through?"

"Oh vividly. Sometimes it haunts her for weeks, months to come."

"So why does she do it?"

"Because she has to," Ferguson told him. "She cannot always tell in advance when she will make contact. We didn't know when we booked your holiday cottage that this is what we would find. In fact we have both been through a very stressful time with a dying relative. We came here in the hope of peace and rest."

"I'm sorry," Ferguson said, looking down at his feet.

"Not your fault."

But Archer's intrigue remained. "Do any other people have these …powers?"

"Some, but I've never met one with powers as acute as Carmel's. She says that to be a successful medium you have to lower your resistance and listen."

"Listen?"

"Not just with your ears," Ferguson said, and then imitating his wife's voice, "but with your very being."

There followed a heavy silence in which Carmel's breathing could be heard.

"So what would you have me do to the cottage – demolish it? Lock the door and throw away the key?" Archer asked, although it was hard to believe the businessman in him was serious about such a proposal.

For all his thrusting commercial ways, he cut a sad figure at that moment. He realised that without an understanding of how the past feeds into the present, he was an empty vessel. He saw that his own failures with son and wife resonated within the building as much as every other human tragedy that had taken place. For all the gut instincts Ferguson possessed about the world of commerce, he was spiritually bereft and knew it.

Ferguson was unable to respond to Archer's question about demolition though it was not clear whether he was expected to. Maybe Archer was hoping for a response from

Carmel, but she remained outside the orbit of human intercourse.

By now she had been moved and was sitting on a kitchen chair. What consciousness manifested itself in her caused her to bend over and moan from deep down. Then she began rubbing her stomach with the palm of her hand.

"Oh, hurt. How it hurts. Oh the pain is deep, deep."

"What's a matter with her?" Archer asked.

"I've no idea," Ferguson said, "I've never seen her like this. Something must have happened while she was in the spirit world."

There came a knock at the door. Both men gave a nervous twitch, as though the dead were now walking and manifesting themselves as living people.

Archer steeled himself sufficiently to open the door.

"Taxi to the railway station for Mr and Mrs Ferguson."

Why, it was none other than Sidney Yedman, formerly occupant of these very premises. Now Sidney was in his own taxi, one of a fleet of four. At home was his wonderful Popsy with the now grown-up twins that seemed such unlikely arrivals at one time.

"We're here," Ferguson said from behind Archer's shoulder to Sidney, "Can you wait for 10 minutes whilst I pack?"

"That's fine, sir, I don't mind spending time in this lovely old house. It was once mine you know."

"You owned it?" Archer exclaimed.

"I believe I was the man you bought it from, Mr Archer."

"Oh, I didn't know it was you."

"I loved this house but only lived here for a short time. My wife felt … out of place."

"Can we focus on getting to the station?" Ferguson asked impatiently, a deeply concerned man.

"Of course, the clock is running."

"Then will you help me get her to the car?" Ferguson added.

Sidney looked past Ferguson to his apparently comatose wife, concerned at what he saw.

"Is she ill, sir?"

"She's er, er, temporarily lost consciousness."

Archer just looked on in wonder. He was awestruck. For him this was a new area of experience. Until now all life had been explainable.

He watched on as Ferguson organised their departure, linking arms with the taxi driver to carry Carmel Ferguson out to the car.

Archer would never be the same again and nor, he suspected, would Carmel Ferguson.

*

CHAPTER EIGHT: *The Writer's Tale*

Following the Ferguson's departure, Archer stood looking out of the window in a kind of stupor until his reverie was broken by the ringing of the phone. He almost took too long to answer; mentally he was coming from so far away.

The voice at the other end of the line was faint and husky. It sounded as though the caller could barely make the effort to call; for all that his demands were stated with conviction. He explained that he was a writer and was looking to book a garret, a hideaway, from which he might complete a project. Archer's accommodation had been recommended to him as somewhere he could 'get away from it all'. He had phoned the town's tourist information bureau and they had given him Archer's phone number at the shop. The girl in charge of the store had passed on this number, the caller continued.

"It's summat I want to arrange as soon as poss," the caller said, as he had a publisher waiting. Archer thought it strange that the caller sounded well-spoken and cultured in some regards, spoke of being a writer, yet had slovenly referred to 'summat' and 'poss'. It was incongruous in the extreme.

At last Archer's mind became focused. The surreal events of the afternoon slipped over the horizon. He was even able to dismiss the smidgen of negative instinct that he felt at the caller. Reason, not instinct, was the way forward for a material man, he figured: business affairs and money matters.

Archer went into business mode. The trauma he had experienced earlier in the day was brushed out of his life with the ease of dust being flicked off his jacket.

“Are you wanting to arrive this week?”

“No later than” the caller rapped out.

“I actually have a cancelled booking on the property I am talking from right now,” he said (pretentiously fostering the notion that he ran a number of holiday homes).

“Sounds good.”

“A client taken ill.” (It wasn’t really a lie).

“It is free from today until the 23rd of the month.”

The caller told him his name was Leonard Broome (‘I’m a Manchester lad’) and he would be on his way within the hour. At that point in time the name Leonard Broome meant no more than John Smith or Colin Brown. It was hardly surprising that Archer was not on his guard; there was nothing to take guard against. But the colloquial manner of the man’s introduction was slightly troubling.

Broome said he would arrive shortly after 8 am that same evening and would pay for the let in cash. Archer told him he would be there to meet him. As soon as he had replaced the receiver he set about tidying the place. The swish of a brush and the hum of the hoover echoed round the building for the next hour. He only stopped what he was doing when he came to the area in front of the casement windows. He had intended to clean the inside of the windows. First he paused as if he was sampling the air. Dismissing any fears he had earlier expressed due to

Carmel Ferguson, he dusted the windows vigorously without another thought.

Archer's reaction to the spiritualist had given me hope that he was after all a man with a soul. Suddenly it seemed he had acquired a depth of vision that he had previously seemed incapable of, but his subsequent actions had revealed him to be a wheeler and dealer with few of the finer sensitivities.

After he had put the inside of the house straight, Archer drove along the A170 to Pickering, keen to close on the day's business at his store and lock up. He was there and back in the space of 90 minutes.

Broome arrived early. He was tall, in his late thirties, possessed a shaved head and classic good looks. Although his blue eyes were deep and penetrating, there was about them a good humour, one that inspired trust. For a man like Broome, his smart appearance and good looks made him dangerous rather than trustworthy. A perfumed odour radiated from him like he had recently bathed in the stuff. He had what might be termed a practised stare. Archer seemed to see none of this. Archer was won over immediately by the sight of fifty pounds as a down payment.

Judge not the man, judge him by the money he wields, would have been Archer's mantra.

"I'll help you bring in any stuff from your car, Mr Broome, if you like. It's a fair walk from the parking place to the front door. I presume you're parked on the river bank."

Broome merely nodded, not really answering Archer's question. He was agreeable to the landlord's suggestion, though somewhat guarded when they reached the car. He handed stuff to Archer from the car's backseat, rather than risk him seeing into the boot.

"If you'll take that lot in," he said in a strong Manchester accent, "I can manage the rest myself."

Archer had been allotted a heavy cardboard box to carry to the front door.

"Thanks for that," Broome said, when he arrived with the trunk, "that's the dog's bollocks – I mean, vital stuff."

"Really?" Archer sounded startled. Once again there was an acute mismatch between Broome's pretensions to be a writer and the coarseness of his tone.

For his part, Broome noticed Archer's attentiveness and conceded some detail.

"The manuscript. That's what my agent is waiting for. I need to finish it during my stay here. Couldn't manage it at home. Too many distractions. You know – other people, phones ringing."

"You *are* a writer then?"

"I am."

He had given away enough, nothing more.

"The box I carried seems very heavy…and you say you've got more to write. It must be some book!"

Broome cleared his throat and even lapsed into a polite chuckle.

"Oh no. What you carried in was only the first draft. Now I have to work at polishing it up for publication.

Second and third draft. Final revision. Burning the midnight oil."

"That's a lot of work. Does it worry you that it might be wasted, that after all that work, it might not be published?" Archer articulated, not even pausing to think that this was none of his business.

Broome stared at him with those deep-set blue eyes, looking more than a little affronted, and answered in uncompromising tones, "Oh, it'll be published all right, don't you worry."

With that, he clicked open a deep blue case, a heavy one that he had carried from the car boot. Out of the case he took a brand new machine.

"Ah, a typewriter," Archer said, "They're German. I've heard about these."

"This one is state of the art," said Broome with, for the first time, a gleam in his eye.

"Very expensive, I believe."

"Very" was all Broome said once inside, pulling a chair up to the table as though he intended to begin work that very minute and giving Archer a shouldn't-you-be-on-your-way glance.

I felt Archer's discomfort. I think he was beginning to realise that here was a man that he would have done well to avoid. Yet it was nothing Broome had said so much as his way of saying it. He was supremely confident. An outsider looking in would have thought Broome the owner of the cottage and Archer the renter. And there were those deep set blue eyes that came from an unrecognisable place.

Archer was no student of human nature, but there was about this man Broome something so profoundly wrong. He had revealed very little of himself yet he possessed the air of a man who was an arch dissembler. Archer had never felt such a sense of unease and therefore had no strategies for dealing with it other than to pretend everything was straightforward.

Broome was easily the most formidable human being who had ever sheltered within my walls: more powerful than Austin Lincoln on the dreadful day of the murder; more intimidating than Monse, (who acted the whole time like he was in charge of everybody and everything around him).

Broome's presence was as disturbing as Carmel Ferguson's. But hers had been a benign presence, his would be perceived as malign by anyone with the equipment to detect it.

"Then I'll leave you to it, Mr Broome," Archer finally said, "or would you prefer to be called Leonard?"

This Broome ignored, his typing fingers already poised over the keys of the typewriter. He countered with a question of his own, "Is there a shop nearby if I have anything I need late at night?"

It was rude and dismissive, but Archer was only too happy to oblige.

"In the village of Seamer, Robinson's stays open till 9 pm" he told him. "It's a grocer's, but they do sweets and newspapers."

"Is there a Post Office?" Broome asked.

"The nearest one is in the same village one along from the grocer's," Archer said. He felt almost compelled to add, "Well, you have my home number if there is anything else you need."

Curiously he dearly hoped that the time would quickly come when this man paid up, got out and never troubled him further. Where Archer's parting question to Broome came from he had no idea, but he soon regretted asking it.

"Are you a well-known writer, Mr Broome. Should I have heard of you?"

Broome looked up with ill-disguised contempt.

"Not yet" was all he said.

Part of Archer wanted to go on and ask him what kind of books he wrote, but something told him that this would be a bridge too far. It struck him that the possibility of violence simmered within Broome.

Archer left and Broome settled down to work. There was no anxiety or nervousness about the man. He adjusted immediately to life within River View Cottage; of all my residents, only Monse had been as at home as this man who claimed to be a writer.

That first evening he set about his business. It was clear that he was working to a plan.

He removed a candle from beneath clothes in the trunk he had carried into the house. He slotted it into a candlestick then looked around for the best place to site it. Unlike other occupants of the cottage, he moved unerringly towards the casement windows. Either he did not possess the awe that others had shown towards that area of the house or, having sensed it, he was unimpressed and refused to be intimidated by it.

The candle was scented and Broome visibly luxuriated in the release of a sweet pleasing odour once the flame had gained momentum. Was it the candle that brought about the transformation that followed?

There was something weird about the man, almost eerie. From a face that was a mask of iron will and almost devilish obsession, he became tranquil, relaxed. His eyes closed and he took deep breaths like one who might be meditating. I saw it then and many times afterwards: he was a man divided. Sometimes deeply troubled, others a being who existed outside the planes of here and now. Almost supernormal. All the secrets of human nature are laid bare when a man is alone in his house; the guards come down.

The script that Broome then took out of the cardboard box, he divided up into eight sections. Once he had done that, he tore open a large brown envelope and out of it he took several photographs. These images he held close to himself, as though afraid that some interloper might get a sight of them, someone looking in from the window say. Then he relaxed and spread the pictures out on a coffee table.

Now he collected the material together into eight distinct piles and appended each group of photos to one of the eight sections of script by use of paperclips. A watcher would have detected both menace and satisfaction in Broome at this activity. As though he was doing something that was secretive and incriminating but at the same time very fulfilling. Occasionally he would pause to examine one of the photographs and his face would relax and absorb the image. What others might refer to as guilty pleasure.

His final act, before settling down for a snooze, was to take a small neat red case out of the bottom of the trunk he had carried in. Nestling inside the case and shining like it had been lovingly polished was a Beretta 70T handgun.

Broome pointed it first in the direction of the TV and made a mock 'bang' noise, then repeated the action but this time targeting the candle in the casement windows. Now he blew on the end of the barrel, as though puffing away imaginary smoke.

Throughout the days that followed, Broome worked tirelessly to knock his manuscript into shape. First he would use pen and pencil to make corrections and annotations then he would scroll a sheet of paper into his typewriter and tap-tap his way to the end of the page. From time to time he would refer to a small notebook that he kept in his leather briefcase.

Inside the case were countless spools of typewriter ribbon which he changed frequently and with dexterity. He wanted his copy to be bold and clear so there would be no doubt about his words and meanings.

He would start the day by going for a walk along the river path and round the village. People spoke morning greetings to him, but he never returned their pleasantries. Upon returning, he would make some breakfast and a pot of coffee, then settle down to a morning's work.

In all the years that people had lived within my space, I had never seen a person so consumed by purpose. He was a man on a mission and it seemed that mission must be completed before he finally departed the sanctuary that I had become.

That was another aspect of Broome that I had seen in no other inhabitant. Monse had been visibly comfortable in my shell, but Broome seemed positively to thrive within my walls. No question, he liked it here. It was as though the resonances of the plague years that Carmel Ferguson had uncovered were of no consequence to such as Broome. Even if he had been aware of those awful years, they would hold no horror for him. Perhaps that was because Broome would usher in his own kind of horror.

Archer stayed away. He was unnerved at the prospect of again confronting his client. Eventually, he had to meet Broome to negotiate further payment and agree a final date. He came on the Friday but Broome would not allow him beyond the front door. He gave Archer another £100 so that he might be allowed to stay on until the Monday of the following week.

"I would find it very difficult to leave on the Sunday" he told Archer, "and there are things I must do on the Monday."

"The next let is due in Monday teatime" Archer told him, "And I need time to tidy up the place for their arrival."

"I will be gone by midday," Broome said, "And you can be sure that that I will leave the house all spic and span for the next people."

Archer pulled a 'sour lemon face' and that was the point at which Broome eased his difficulties with the passing of five twenty-pound notes for the extended stay.

That final weekend saw River View Cottage turned into a hive of activity: typing, checking, collating and finally, on the Sunday evening, packing the entire manuscript and photographs into a neat brown paper parcel. On top of everything, in an envelope of its own, was a letter typed by Broome directly to the literary agent.

Broome rose early on the Monday morning, tidying up the house as best he could. After making himself cereal, toast and coffee for breakfast, he put the parcel he had prepared for posting under his arm and set out for the Post Office at Seamer. It was just gone 9 am.

At the Post Office, he asked the young counter clerk if she could make up sufficient postage to ensure that the package arrived in London next morning. He accepted proof of posting, but waved away the idea that the parcel needed to be signed for at the other end. His erratic manner, personal charm mixed with a barely contained short-temperedness ensured that she would remember him in the future when the police later made their enquiries.

Finally, Broome made a quick call at the garage to buy a can of paraffin before returning to the cottage.

*

CHAPTER NINE: *The Agent's Tale*

Houses wait without expectation. That is what they do. Everything about them is determined by the people who live in them. Houses may store memories and hoard atmosphere, but their state is passive. Sometimes neurotic people believe that they are at the mercy of their environment, that houses can seal their fate. But a house can only change in a manner that is cosmetic and inflicted by man: a door frame here, a new bathroom and a lick of paint there, a reconstructed chimney stack, a new layer of roof tiles.

A person may change how they feel about a house, how they are affected by it, but in truth the house is a constant. So the relationship can only change on account of an alteration, for good or bad, in the perception of the one who dwells within.

There are people who become afraid and unhappy in a place that once protected them and offered protection; a place they at first called home. Until the unexpected threat came. Then there are homes that were taken on purely as respite, temporary shelter. Circumstances can turn such shelters into sanctuaries, stations for the soul.

And yet a house is not an accident of nature like a tree or a valley…everything about a house has been hewn from nature by man. It has been moulded, shaped, pressed and finally determined by his hands.

I was an extension of the thoughts and feelings of those men who five hundred years ago built me as a place of worship. Eventually men drifted away from me. I was neither home to them nor did I meet the needs of dwellers in the valley. Fenby and Ashcroft saw a ruined building that they could renovate into something of value. They were impressed by neither form nor purpose, but saw worth in the materials from which I was constructed.

They subverted my purpose, turning my architecture to an alternative, more earthly use. All those that dwelled within my space from then on became intimidated by an atmosphere of malice, victims of my imagined powers. Yet they knew nothing of me; even mistaking my origins. Railway cottage indeed!

Broome was no such person. He was the most determined man who had ever existed within my walls. Far from being a victim, he created victims. Broome was never in thrall to me. The man did not know the meaning of apprehension and never considered that a house could hold a person in fear. No, I was to be his plaything, the final part of a terrible plan he had hatched over days, weeks, months, years even.

Do people make houses or do houses make people? River Cottage was the sum of all the people and events that had occurred in a particular place on a tiny insignificant planet. What I had become as a result of all the interactions within my shell suited Broome down to the ground. How could he have known of my history? Coming from a hundred miles away was it just a lucky strike? Or was he of the same stuff as my most terrible events, drawn to me by an indefinable thread?

It was Monday morning. This was to be the culmination of his writing holiday; the day on which he slotted into place the final piece of his awful jigsaw. Yet, for the first time in his stay, his expression became anxious.

He made himself another cup of coffee and smoked two Camel cigarettes. He turned on the radio loud enough to drown thought. It seemed like his own company had finally proved too much for him.

Finally, stubbing out his last cigarette, he rose decisively from the table. After listening to the weather he turned off the radio. In view of what was to follow it was impossible to understand what import the weather could possibly have for him.

Things went deathly quiet. He went out to his car and returned carrying the can of paraffin.

Unscrewing the top off the can, he sloshed the paraffin everywhere. Upstairs, downstairs. On the furniture, the carpet and the curtains. Soon its smell was so intense that its fumes caused him to stumble around drunkenly. He laughed hysterically, cried histrionic tears and shouted at the top of his voice. Like the paraffin, his feelings were being spilled everywhere.

He reopened the battle-scarred trunk he had bought with him and from it he took a bottle of scotch and poured its contents into half a tankard that he had found in the kitchen cupboard. He supped it with the desperation of a thirsty man and then sat down to let it take effect.

Sitting in the armchair of his holiday home, he cast a critical eye at every wall, every corner of the room. Previously he had shown no interest in the building; it was just a garret, a hideaway from the world, a place of concealment whilst he completed his precious manuscript. Now he stared at every nook and cranny as though he was consumed by his interest in his temporary home, noticing it for the first time.

But it was more than that. I could sense this much about him. He was about to destroy everything, including himself. He had no awareness of the faded bloodstain on my floor, of the outside lavatory where a woman had killed herself, of casement windows that had sheltered the dead and dying for nights on end, the child's grave out in the garden. Whatever had been my effect on human beings who had dwelled within my walls, Broome was a person beyond my reach. So steeped in evil and selfish purpose was this man that I was unremarkable in his terrible universe. I was simply a place, any place, where he must do what he had set out to do.

He returned to the trunk for one final time, to remove two items: the Biretta handgun and a box of matches. Now I knew his game.

Despite that drunkenness had set in, he moved with the stealth of a hunted animal. Bounding up the stairs, he lit matches, ensured each had a lusty flame and dropped them on carpets, on furniture, in bedrooms and on the landing. Down the stairs at a pace, he repeated his fire-raising in the kitchen and the living room.

His generosity with the fuel meant that flame and heat soon engulfed my walls causing me to spit and hiss and scream and buckle and bend with the torture of it all.

Oh how I was consumed by flame, dear reader. The reds and blues, the yellows and greens; all colours fed into my funeral pyre. How the flames danced and how the fabric of the building screamed. Truly, it was a thing of terrible beauty.

Then my tortured walls surrendered every memory. The face of every plague victim glowed above the seething mass. There was Ashcroft with his split skull; Austin Lincoln with the mulberry-stained noose marks around his neck. Richard Binns and his father appearing as lifeless corpses with unstoppable water trickling from their silent mouths. Joan Groves' body shivering its final parody of a dance at the end of a rope.

In the midst of the conflagration there was the sharp crack of a handgun. But there were no witnesses to the end of Broome's life, so swiftly had the fire taken hold. His plan was now perfect, the mystery complete. He would never be touched by the unspeakable torture of the fire's searing heat. He had swapped that terror for the cold clinical bullet to the brain. A short sharp knowledge of death that lasted a fleeting fraction being preferred over minutes of insufferable agonising heat.

What was left of him would be unidentifiable even by his dental records. And that, of course, was exactly what his love of mystery demanded. That was the master-stroke of his plan. He knew well how humankind would revile him once it heard his story so he would have to light his own candle. This way the story would unfold according to Leonard Broome's script. Make them piece it together along his lines. Even in death he would have a small victory.

This pistol shot was his final, most awful deed. What he had set in motion would lead people to conclude that Leonard Broome had perished in a consuming fire at a location in which he had made his final confession. But there would be scant evidence of his death. Not even one bone or a tooth. Just a legend.

Best that everyone forget I ever existed, the letter accompanying his script would say, knowing full well that his confession would render that impossible.

There was no delay in reporting the fire at River View Cottage, so ferociously did it burn. The fire brigade covered the four miles in record time. They unfurled their hoses and trained them on the upstairs windows, knowing gravity would pull the water downwards.

I hissed and spat my displeasure, windows exploded and hungry flames tongued the air through the openings. Now they pumped the river water and the fire's ferocity was finally doused. Ladders were laid against the wall and men scuttled up them. I sighed and groaned as smoke and hot damp air displaced the angry spiralling vortex of fire that had inflicted such hurt. By the evening of the day it was clear that the damage was severe. Only the shell of the house was saved. Some of the ground floor stonework proved very resilient – a testimony to its ancient strength.

Valuable time was spent and human life risked at assessing whether the building was inhabited. Later, at the coroner's inquest, two of the firemen who ventured into the building to search for bodies would give hesitant accounts that they had seen indefinable forms, possibly human, moving through the flames.

"Not very likely that anything survived" the coroner would say, "the man whose remains were found almost certainly ended his life before the fire took hold. A bullet had pierced the pan of his brain."

Until Archer arrived at the scene, it was thought by the fire chief that the conflagration had been the result of an electrical fault or an accident involving a candle.

Called by the police, the devastated expression on Archer's face was there for all to see.

"I trust you were insured, sir?" the Chief Fire Officer asked.

"Yes, yes, it was a holiday let."

"A holiday let? Was anyone staying in it?"

"Yes. He said he would leave by midday. Promised me the house would be ready for the next people."

"It'll be a long time before there are any next people, sir."

Archer gave them Leonard Broome's name and when the heat had dispersed sufficiently for firemen to enter what was left of the building, they raked through the ashes and unearthed the heat-buckled metal framework of a typewriter and the butt of a handgun. One of them found the scorched remains of the skull.

"He was a writer," Archer told them, "Booked this place so he could complete a project…for his agent."

"A writer of what, sir? Novels?"

"Didn't say. Didn't say much at all. Of course, I didn't know anything about the gun. He never mentioned it."

Archer gave them Broome's contact details, an address that proved wholly false.

"Said he came from Manchester," Archer told them.

A search of the appropriate data bases found just one Leonard Broome in the wider area. He was in his late seventies and a police visit found him restlessly wandering a Macclesfield dementia home wearing a Stetson hat. Police intelligence ruled him out immediately.

Having drawn a blank, the enquiry started from a new point: the motor car that had been abandoned in the Cock and Feathers car park. A weird and quite unpredictable thread emerged but it took several weeks to unravel the man's identity.

The car was traced to one Leonid Anton Bromski. He had been born of an émigré Russian father and an English mother. He had lived with his aged mother in a quiet Chesire cul-de-sac and worked from home as an accountant. The house was jam-packed with literary works and books of great photographers. The 92 year old mother was in a state of confusion, but still managing to take care of her own basic needs.

"Is Lenny working away?" she asked, "he's always off somewhere."

As aged as the mother was, she was in full possession of her senses. The incredible story fell from her lips effortlessly. Her wonderful son Lenny had been treated terribly by his Russian father. Even the slightest trespass as a child caused her husband to fasten up young Leonid by a chain. He was kept outside in a dog kennel for days on end and often made to bark for his food.

"Why didn't you step in and demand that your husband stop this?" they asked her.

She looked down her glasses in a pitying way "You say that with no knowledge of the kind of man my husband was. He was a Jew in Russia and was captured by the Nazis and tortured terribly. He managed to escape and came to England. I thought him a gentle and concerned man…till I married him. He had been turned into an animal, a crazy animal."

"So how did this end?" they asked her.

"My son grew bigger and stronger. He outgrew his chains. His father's dominance was challenged. One day I heard the sounds of an argument followed by a silence that stayed in the air and I knew something terrible had occurred.

"He got rid of his father's body. Don't ask me how or where."

"How long ago was that?"

"Perhaps twenty years. Shortly after that, my Leonid announced to me – 'Mother' he said. 'I am going to tell the world that from now on my name is no longer Leonid Bromski. From now I will call myself Leonard Broome. I do not want to be known as a Russian'."

For several hours after the fire had burned out Archer had stayed outside the building. He could not bear to enter the charred remains. His feelings were too raw. If only…he had listened to Carmel Ferguson.

"Is there anything left of him – the bloke who called himself Leonard Broome – inside the house?"

"Just dust, sir, and the scorched remains of his skull and skeleton. Nothing we could use to identify him."

Unaccountably, Archer spoke up. "I know someone who might be able to help you."

"Help us, sir?" said the police officer, a tall moustachioed man, with tombstone teeth.

"Help you find out about the bloke – Leonard Broome, or whoever he was. She'll tell you stuff about the house too."

The policeman fingered his moustache. "Stuff about the house? You mean how it caught fire?"

Archer realised how stupidly he had bungled. Carmel Ferguson would probably refuse to have anything more to do with him after the warning she had given. In any case, the thought of the police or fire people turning to a psychic for help was ludicrous.

"I meant – this is a house with a history. A lot of strange – bad – things have happened in it over the years. She seems to know a lot about them is all," he said, waffling painfully through his explanation.

The policeman exchanged pained expressions with the chief fire officer.

"Was this lady – I think you said it was a lady – actually on the premises with this Leonard Broome character?"

Archer bit the bullet. "She's a psychic. She and her husband had a let on this place before Broome so 'No' they never met him. They left the house because they were disturbed by it."

“Disturbed? By who, sir?”

“Not ‘who’, officer, ‘what’. She was upset by the house. She said there was something very disturbing about the building. Said it had been an old church.”

“I thought it was an old railway cottage…”

“That’s what everyone thinks…but it’s not apparently.”

“This lady – what was her name?” the fire officer asked.

“Carmel Ferguson. She didn’t come from round here.”

“Did she have any fact-based information? Did she have reason to suspect that the place might catch fire? Did she think Broome might be an arsonist?”

“None of that,” Archer said, “I told you she was a psychic. I should have listened to her. She told me to lock the door and go away. Said the house would only bring trouble. But I didn’t listen. Soon as they’d gone, her and her husband, I let the place to Broome.”

“Hmmm” said the policeman, “It sounds like Mrs Ferguson is someone we should talk to – just to cover all our options.”

“Eh?” Archer asked incredulously.

“Perhaps she kept something to herself, Mr Archer. It all sounds a bit fishy. We have a dead man to account for. We can’t take it lightly.”

Archer felt uneasy that he may have dropped an innocent woman into a mess not of her making. But events two hundred miles away in London in that same week provided answers to the mystery of the burning house and there was never need to involve Carmel Ferguson.

Very little evidence came from the scene of the crime. For one thing, the house was fire-damaged almost beyond recognition and unlikely to yield any evidence of criminal activity. For another, the identity of the arsonist could not be established...all that was salvaged by the fire crew was the remnant of a skull. The abandoned car became their only lead and in that pre-computer age it took several weeks to track down the car log and establish ownership. In those days, DNA technology did not exist so identification by that route was not possible...and then Broome's confession was revealed by a London literary agent, who realised immediately she had the hottest script in town.

Five minutes into reading the script a quick glance through the accompanying photographs was enough to convince her that the package, if authentic, was publishing dynamite.

Her next thought was that several agents had probably received copies of this same script in an effort to promote a bidding war, but when she read Broome's letter that was clearly not the case. First of all it told her that the sender was no longer alive. That despatching this parcel was the penultimate act of his life. And then there was this -

We met once at a media function in Manchester, Ms Jameson, do you remember? We had a long conversation about the rights and wrongs of publishing. Some BBC idiot asked you whether there were limits to what should be published. You told him there were two criteria: truth and literary merit. I thought that was an excellent answer. My script gives you the opportunity to stand by your words. I assure you every word of my story is true and I think the writing is not without style and merit.

Her memory of this meeting was dim and distant, but there had been her and two or three men. It was at a Manchester hotel. Rather than anything said, she remembered being struck by the almost dazzling blueness of one of the party's eyes. He must have been the one. She shivered inwardly later at the thought that a serial killer had used a chance meeting to track her details down, even if the net result could bring her untold riches.

Much as she would have loved to have gone ahead and contacted a publisher who would have snatched off her hand for such a sensational project, she had no option but to hand it over to the law. Of course, knowing what an ass the law can be, she made her own facsimile before handing it over. Now she had evidence on which she could arouse press interest.

Don't go for those sleazy red tops, she thought, go for a broadsheet that would give the story due gravitas.

On the morning of April 4th 1977, the story hit the headlines in *The Times.*

CANDLELIGHT KILLER: PUBLISH AND BE DAMNED?

Antonia Graham (Crime Correspondent)

Literary agent Stella Jameson may be in possession of the greatest publishing coup of the decade if not century or she could be about to enter a legal minefield.

Leonard Broome, the self-styled 'Candlelight Killer' chose Jameson as the recipient for his sensational confession. Quite why Broome selected the London agent is not clear, but what she has is a 60,000 word confession of a notorious serial killer complete with photographs taken at the scene of each crime.

Between 1967 and 1973 eight children vanished from locations in Northern England. The bodies were subsequently discovered at various countryside locations by members of the public. Police knew that these murders were the work of a single killer because a lit candle had been placed next to each child together with a message in an envelope. The contents of the envelope, believed to be the same in each case, were never made public by the police at the time.

In the autobiographical work posted to Jameson, Broome claimed to be the killer and took pictures at each crime scene.

"I have only the slimmest connection with Leonard Broome," Ms Jameson told me, "but he makes it clear in the accompanying letter who the script was intended for… me."

There are problems with publication. Should anyone profit from publicity about such horrendous murders? What good would publication serve? Could Broome's killings become the focus of public attention? The photographs, whilst being an essential component of the document and convincing proof as to the murderer's identity would surely cause unnecessary suffering to the families concerned.

"I think Broome was himself torn in two by his own actions," Jameson said, "the letter he sent accompanying the confession made it clear that all profits from the publication should go to the NSPCC. He was a latter day Jekyll and Hyde. He wanted people to understand how he lost his way during his own childhood and to increase their understanding of serial killers."

"He was a warped and twisted mind who himself had a sick childhood," she went on, "but only by studying his thinking and his modus operandi can we come to terms with what he did. The book is a valuable insight into a psychopath's mind and not to publish would deprive the world and criminologists in particular of an important historic document."

It is believed that Broome died in a house fire at an undisclosed location in North Yorkshire in August last year. Police have remained tight-lipped about details of Broome's death, but it is thought that if publication of Broome's confession goes ahead unanswered questions about his death will come to light.

*

CHAPTER TEN: *The Entrepreneur's Tale*

St Mary's, the church from which first I came, was all that was left of me now. The terrible heat from the fire had claimed everything except the basic brick and stone work and even that was burned and scorched almost beyond recognition. Once the demolition crews had made me safe, I was a mere shell of what I once had been, with a scorched concrete floor and stars and sky where the roof had sat.

And so I remained through autumn and winter: an eyesore, a place to avoid. There were numerous complaints to the council that I ruined the old world charm. I was a sign of something rotten at the heart of the village.

Archer himself went into decline. Wracked by an absurd sense of guilt for bringing Broome into the community, it was as though part of him felt responsible for the child murders his tenant had carried out. Archer had no close friends, but his business contacts sympathised with him and told him that what had occurred could have happened to anyone. It was sheer misfortune, they said. This was of scant comfort to Archer; he could not escape the feeling that he had been punished for his poor judgment in allowing Broome to use the house after Carmel Ferguson's warning. He looked on his life now as a series of misadventures brought about by his own chronic misjudgment rather than plain bad fortune. He hated himself so long and hard that it hurt in a place deep in his stomach.

Just a month after the fire, he returned to his flat above the shop one evening to discover that Lincoln, the dog that had been such a good companion since the departure of his wife and son, had died during the day. The sadness he felt was overwhelming and out of proportion, but it felt like a final nail. The sense that he was on an irreversible downward spiral accelerated.

Reinforced by the dark winter days, Archer's gloom turned into depression. His thoughts turned to the son he had not seen for years in the vague hope of finding some consolation, someone who cared and could empathise, but he lacked the courage to confront his estranged wife.

Suddenly his business issues did not matter one jot. Instead of launching himself into the restoration of River View Cottage as a project, (as he would have done ten years earlier), he now resented the fact that the cursed house was always there – at the back of his mind – something that he could neither overlook nor deal with.

His health took a turn for the worse. Nausea set in. The very thought of food set up a reaction. He would vomit on at least three occasions most days. In the aftermath of the fire he would visit the house almost daily, desperate to conceive of a plan for restoring it. Now, suffering from depression and poor health, he turned his back on River View Cottage and adopted an 'out of sight, out of mind' attitude.

A doctor's examination confirmed a diagnosis even his worst fears had not anticipated: a primary cancer of the stomach.

"I hope we have caught it in time, Mr Archer," his doctor said. "I'm a great believer in the power of positive thought," the GP went on, "but you seem very distracted. I wondered whether worry was playing a part in your illness."

It was true. Archer experienced constant distraction. It gnawed away at him like a rodent insinuating its teeth into his soft tissue. He would wake in the middle of the night, visit the toilet and fight against wakefulness without success once he returned to bed. Closing his eyes, instead of seeing the darkness of velvet night as a backdrop to further sleep, he saw a black twisted stump of a building on the inside of his eyelids.

He tried to explain the night time difficulties to his doctor. It was hard. He was not used to detailing personal weakness.

"The ruins of my cottage, the one that burned down," he opened, "they haunt my dreams and nag my days like a bad toothache."

"Everyone's troubles are magnified to the power of ten at three in the morning," the GP tried to reassure him with his soft Irish tones.

The question 'And what do they do about it?' formed in his head, but it stayed there. The sleeping tablets prescribed brought not one jot of relief.

The publication of *The Candlelight Killer* had now cleared all of the legal hurdles and, more than two years after the fire, was ready for publication. Archer was full of dread that when the book was finally published, the story of the events at River View Cottage would thrust him into the limelight. People would know for sure that Broome had stayed in the property he owned and that he, Archer, had been instrumental in events.

Police and legal teams had been closely involved with the publishers to find an acceptable publication format: one that did not sensationalise Broome's terrible crimes or cause the victims' families 'undue pain'. Despite her own worsening health issues Stella Jameson stood to become a rich woman on the basis of one 'lucky find' and the previews were coming thick and fast in the quality press. The public appetite for what would be a huge best-seller was being readied.

The Parish Council was now besieged by complaints from locals who felt the fire-blasted building should be demolished. It was a magnet to local youths, a scar on the local environment, a place shrouded in fear and mystery that attracted the grubbier elements of society.

By now the rumour had been launched that a serial killer had sheltered here. Once the full story got out, who could tell what the repercussions might be? (The conventional wisdom was that Broome had taken fright at the evil forces at work within my walls, confessed all in his book and then committed suicide by setting fire to the building.)

As time passed and Archer remained inactive in the matter, the council considered a compulsory purchase order. Then Archer's health nose-dived into a serious decline. The radiotherapy was making no impression on the growth; demise and death at the relatively young age of 53 followed. Another name was added to the list of the victims attributed to my innate evil and more tongues were set wagging.

Young Norman Archer could barely remember his father, but was most pleasantly surprised to find himself the sole beneficiary of Frederick's will. His mother was still alive and not at all disappointed with having no mention in Archer's will.

"The less I have to do with your father, dead or alive, the better."

Norman looked at his inheritance and scratched his head at the description in the will of River View Cottage in all its dilapidation. He asked his mother about its history. She told Norman what she knew of the cottage, concluding with its destruction by fire.

"The best thing you can do is level it and sell off the raft of land to a builder. Lots of people looking for a nice house next to a river, if you ask me."

Which Norman didn't. Instead he asked her if she would come with him to have a look at what remained of the cottage. They arrived one Saturday afternoon in a sports car he had bought with some of his father's money.

They stood among the ruins and, in view of the grim surroundings and his mothers' cynicism, held a surprisingly civilised conversation.

"Do you think the place was cursed, mother?"

"Well, it certainly didn't bring us any happiness."

"What did father think?"

"At first he said it was his dream house. He loved the idea of living next to a river. Even so, he moved out soon after we left and turned it into a holiday home. What does that tell you?"

"That it held bad memories for him?"

"Sometimes, when we first lived there, he used to say that he could hear the house talking."

"Was he going insane?"

"I don't know, Norman. I asked him what things it was saying and all he would answer was that its voice came from long ago. 'If you're so upset by the house, why have you brought us here?' I once asked him."

"And what did he say?"

"The oddest answer. He said that it didn't upset him, it excited him. Besides, he said, he had always wanted to live in a house out in the country next to a river."

Norman stood and looked at the husk that I had become for quite some time. It was getting unbearably cold and snow was threatening. His focus switched to the garden.

"It looks like that tree's had it," he said, pointing to the laburnum.

"Don't say that. Your dad loved it."

"Looks half dead to me. Must have got scorched by the blaze. I'll have to get somebody in to take it out."

How his father had loved the bright golden flowers on the tree Binns had planted long ago.

"I'll keep that oak tree" he said "very unusual."

"Your dad thought it strange. The double oak, he called it."

Both of them stood staring at it, unaware of how it came to be there.

"It's about time we went back to the car," his mother said.

"Hmm, I don't quite know what I'm going to do with this place," young Norman said, enjoying the feel of control the words gave him.

"Do the same as you're planning with that laburnum tree," his mother insisted, "Knock the damn thing down is what I say."

"That would be a shame to lose the lot," he said, "even now I can see what its appeal was for my father."

"Blessed if I can," his mother said, regarding him with some trepidation.

Norman screwed up his eyes and looked at his 'pile' as though he was trying to read something into it. Margaret was quiet and patient, as she always was with her boy, the one decent result of her unhappy marriage.

"I think I have an idea," Norman said, "quite a crazy little scheme, but it might make us some money."

"Us?"

"Of course, mother. You didn't think I would just cut you out of father's riches, did you? After what he put you through you are entitled to some rights and I'll respect them."

Supported by his father's money, Norman had eventually gone to private school. It had been the only way for Frederick to make sure his son got out from under his mother's feet and influence and received an education. He had insisted upon the venture and funded it generously. Indeed, he had never missed a parents' evening. Although not a shining academic star, Norman had gone on to business school and perhaps inherited some of his father's commercial nous.

After leaving business school, Norman had started to buy up housing stock in rundown areas of town, using a small team of reliable workers to restore the dwellings with sanitation, plumbing and electricity. After an initial struggle, he was now a landlord collecting rent from several properties.

River View might have seemed a heaven-sent opportunity, but his small team of artisans had never been used on the kind of rebuilding project he now envisaged. Besides, his ingenious plan did not involve turning it into a rent or a holiday let. No, he had a much greater work in mind and to achieve it he would need to do a good deal of research and recruit other interested parties.

He began that very day, the minute he had dropped off his mother at her flat. He turned the car round and headed back the way he had come. His port of call was the Cock and Feathers, not the busiest of places just before Saturday teatime. The front door was open and there was a smell of bacon frying, but the lounge was empty. Nor could he hear any activity in the public bar. He shouted for assistance, but none came. It would have been the easiest thing in the world to nip behind the bar and help himself.

'They deserve no less' he thought 'what a rural backwater this village is.' And yet there existed a busy holiday town just four miles away.

To get attention, he picked up a beer mat and hammered it forcefully on the bar. The publican emerged from an unexpected opening, the cellar door, and Norman jumped with surprise.

"What can I get you, young sir?"

"I'll have a JD, please?"

"A JD, sir?"

"Jack Daniels on the rocks, please."

As the barman scooped the pitiful excuse for ice out of the bucket, Norman asked him:

"Are you the landlord here?"

"I am. Jack Hamshaw."

"Ah, a Hamshaw. I think your family have owned this pub for a long time?"

"Oh we have, sir, we go way back. I don't own it now though, the brewery does. It's a managed house."

"So, being a local with such roots, do you know much about the history of the village?"

"Quite a bit. Why?"

"I wanted to find someone who could go way back. A hundred years or so…"

"We don't have anybody that old still alive," the barman said, pouring the whisky and keeping a face as rigid as a rock.

"Who's the oldest living person in the village?"

"That'll be Peggy Prince. She's into her nineties. Grand old dear. Still got all her marbles an' all."

"Could you give me her address?"

"I don't think she'll talk to you, sir, without someone else being present. Someone she knows. Understandably, quite nervous. Programmes about crime on the telly affect old people these days."

"In that case, is there someone who knows her that I could talk to?"

"Can I ask is it anything in partic'lar you want to talk to her about?"

Archer realised there was no point in hiding his purpose. This man was a gatekeeper and would never let him through without full details.

"My dad was Frederick Archer. He was the owner of River View. He's died and I've inherited it. I'd like to do some work on the house, but first I want to get a full picture."

"Best thing you can do with that rubble heap is knock the bugger down." Here Hamshaw paused, sensing the opportunity for a bit of salacious gossip.

"Is there anything in these stories that have been in the papers about this serial killer Leonard Broome who's supposed to have stayed there?"

"Yes, I do know about the man. A lot'll come out when his book's published."

"Made people in the village very nervous, that business did."

"But I remember my dad saying that lots of weird stuff had happened in River View long before that," said Norman Archer, heading the landlord off at the pass.

Of course, this was not strictly true for he had barely spoken to his dad in the last 10 years of his life. Most of what he did know about the cottage came from his mother.

"Well, you're in luck. My gran – Molly – she's a good friend of Mrs Prince. If I introduce you I'm sure that'll get you what you want. These old girls, they like nowt better than a good chin-wag about the old times."

From the wimpish, self-indulgent child his mother had encouraged, Norman Archer had developed into quite a savvy operator. Although very much a mummy's boy, he knew just what to keep private and what to put on public display.

Jack Hamshaw fixed him up with an audience with Molly Hamshaw and Peggy Prince the following Monday evening. For Norman's part he knew how to charm old ladies and for their part they enjoyed the company of a good-looking if somewhat chubby young man who constantly flattered to deceive.

There were no written records for him to draw on, but the oral history they passed on to him was both detailed and colourful and he recorded it all in a bright red notebook. At the centre of the epic tale was the murderer, Austin Lincoln. 'A man who hanged and lived to tell the tale' was how his notes later described it.

"It's no surprise that 'orrible man who killed little children came to live at t'cottage," Peggy told him, "the story of that place starts with a murderer – the man who planned t'house. They called him Austin Lincoln, he were a drunk and a psycho, but they say he were a clever man."

It was Molly Hamshaw who filled in the details about Fenby and Ashcroft and how Lincoln came into the mix. Norman couldn't scribble quickly enough.

Peggy jumped in with the juiciest part of the tale: how Lincoln escaped the hangman's noose and 'made his way back to t'scene of t'crime.'

“While the hangman couldn’t do for him, the cottage could,” and she explained how his skeleton had been found months after his death on the house floor.

“So what actually killed him in the end?” Norman asked.

“No one knows,” Peggy told him in a voice that trailed off, “there was summat about him being poisoned, though they never knew what with or who by. So it’s said.”

“Didn’t do post mort-hims in those days” Molly added.

“They called him Lincoln Austin you say? That’s funny” said Norman, “my dad had a little dog called Lincoln.”

“There’s been more than one dog in that house,” Mrs Prince told him. “There was one barked day and night because his owner had been killed by a flying slate.”

“A flying slate?” Norman repeated incredulously.

“True. It were me that reported the matter. Oh too many years ago to remember. Well, we told the bobbies and they found him. Been lying there ages and t’dog was at point of starvation.”

“And who was this man who got killed?” Norman asked, pen and notebook poised.

“The one who got slated you mean? He were an actor. I can’t remember what they called him, but it were in t’paper at the time.”

“Name were Monse,” Molly chipped in helpfully.

Norman was aware that he was getting a comprehensive account of previous life in his newly acquired property, but that it totally lacked chronology.

"Who was the first person ever to live in the house – do you know?" he asked.

Peggy took up the story again, telling of the terrible fate of the Binns family.

"Lord Huntley brought them 'ere. Binns was a top gardener over at Castle Howard. I believe cottage were built specially for him, but Binns's wife never liked it. She wasn't of these parts. Some said she were a gyppo."

"Young son Richard drowned in t'river and they blamed his mother. Said she weren't keeping an eye on 'im. They say there was an awful row between t'parents with each blaming t'other."

"Family buggered off back to Malton. Isn't that what happened, Pegs?" Molly interjected.

"Aye, but not the husband, he didn't. He stayed on as the gardener. He didn't go. He wasn't welcome cos t'marriage were over. He stayed at t'cottage on his own and one day not long after my great grandfather found his body in t'river, bobbing up an' down like a dead cow."

"That was two of 'em dead by drowning, him and his son," Molly added. "People were already blaming the house and saying it were cursed."

"So that made four dead in all," Peggy pointed out with a grim nod of satisfaction.

"There were more?" Norman asked.

"Oh aye" Peggy said, "We're getting towards modern times now."

"There were a couple of lesbians living there just before the war, weren't there, Peggy?"

"I can remember their names – Mary Ford and Joan Groves. Ford woman were a niece or summat of the bloke named Monse who had lived there on his own. The one who were killed by a slate one windy night. They said he were some kind of actor. Wore a weird black hat and he had a dog too.

"It went all right, these lesbian lovers, then one of them took up with a young chap from town. She must have been one of them transsexuals…" Peggy continued.

"Yer mean bisexual," Molly pushed in.

"I don't know all these modern terms. It was all just straightforward in my day," Peggy said as though she was a dead person talking.

"Anyroad…she went and hung herself," Molly added.

"In the house?" Norman asked, feigning shock and amazement..

"No, in t'outhouse. They didn't find her body for ages."

"That were five dead altogether now," Peggy put in.

Now Molly made a big play for attention. With a powerful sense of dramatic timing, she took the stage: "Hold on! Hold on!"

Peggy and Norman focused on her.

"A woman came in t'pub not so long back. Just before that child murderer business. She were full of it. Said the 'ouse weren't a railway 'ouse at all. Said it were an old church."

"Can you remember her name?" Norman asked.

"Well, I can't, but I bet young Jack will at t'pub. It were his dad, my son, that dealt with her. They practically chucked her out the pub from what I remember."

"Why on earth did she say it had been a church? I mean, what grounds did she have for that?"

"Search me" Peggy said.

The evening finished with a cup of tea made by Norman. After a few minutes he thanked his hostesses and made his way back to the Cock and Feathers. He guessed that the oldish fellow behind the bar must have been the Hamshaw Molly referred to.

"Excuse me, are you Jack's dad?"

"I am that. Gordon Hamshaw's the name."

Norman explained who he was, where he had just been and how the meeting had come to a prompt but not entirely satisfactory conclusion.

"Do you remember the woman you ejected from the pub, Mr Hamshaw?"

"I'm not likely to forget her or her husband in a hurry, although I didn't actually chuck them out. That's mother being a drama queen.

"Very highly strung woman, she was. Had some crazy ideas about your dad's house. We all knew it were an old railway cottage but she said it had been a church. Full of fancy ideas. She was upsetting my customers."

"Can you remember her name?"

"That I can't. She had her husband with her. I can allus remember a face, but names just pass me by."

"Hmmm, any ideas about where she came from or how I can contact her? I need to know for some research I'm doing."

"Well, didn't Mr Archer – your dad that is – have some kind of guest book? By law they have to keep a record, don't they? My advice would be to leave the woman alone. She looked like a piece of work to me."

Archer pretended to weigh up Hamshaw's words, nodding sagely, then drank up and left.

At first he had thought Hamshaw's suggestion about a guest book sound, but then the thought occurred to him that any such document would have been a casualty of the fire.

He had reached what felt like a dead end. This guest who had upset the applecart all that time ago was the missing link. Without input from her, his brilliant idea would never be realised. He decided to share his frustrations with his mother.

"Well, of course your father kept a guest book, Norman," she told him, "He was many things, yer dad – most of them bad – but he was meticulous about stuff like that."

"Is it still around?"

"About two weeks after his death a policeman brought round a bag of stuff from your dad's flat. Most of it was rubbish, but I did take the trouble to go through it before I ditched it."

"So are you saying there was a guest book among it?"

"Yes. I think your dad met people as they arrived, made them sign the book and then kept it in his flat."

Norman no longer lived with his mum so he was surprised when she produced the precious book from a high shelf in the pantry.

"One of the main reasons I kept it was because the last entry was that Leonard Broome. The police checked it. Never know, it might be worth something one day."

Norman was more shocked than surprised at his mother's coldly calculating attitude. She was talking in such matter of fact terms about an item that linked a serial child killer and the death of her own estranged husband. He didn't know whether to admire or despise her for such a cold and calculating attitude.

"Here is the contact I'm after" he said, copying down the Birmingham address of Carmel Ferguson.

"What do you want that for?" his mother asked, a note of outrage in her voice.

"The final piece of the jigsaw," he said.

"What jigsaw?"

"That's for me to know and you to find out about."

She looked at him inquisitively.

"All in the fullness of time, mother."

*

CHAPTER ELEVEN: *The Husband's Tale*

The journey down to Birmingham was treacherous. Snow had been falling for the last 24 hours and Norman's 'beamer' did not have the best grip in icy conditions. It was with relief that he finally pulled off the motorway and headed for the Sparkbrook area of the city. It took several stops and enquiries of locals who trudged miserably through the sludge of a grim winter's day before he found Oldfield Road.

The Fergusons' place was an unprepossessing semi-detached house with a decent-sized front garden that had gone to seed. Norman Archer knocked twice, a sound that resonated in the hallway and reinforced the idea that the house's inhabitants had gone away.

After a couple of minutes' wait he shuffled disappointedly through the slush back to his car, feeling the day had been an absolute waste. He had just turned the key to release the driver door when he heard behind him the withdrawing of bolts and the turning of a doorknob. A man in his late fifties with an unkempt appearance and a look of disappointment strewn across his features, stared into the deserted street beyond Norman. That struck him as strange. There was no attempt at eye contact.

"I was looking for a Carmel Ferguson," Norman said.

"Not here anymore," the man said, raising his hand and wiping the back of it on his lips.

"That's a shame" Norman answered, "Has she moved house? Do you know where she lives now?"

"I'm her husband," the man said, his face still conveying utter misery.

Now Norman was at a disadvantage and felt acute embarrassment. Had he stumbled upon a marital break-up? How did he explain why he wanted to talk to this man's wife?

"Carmel's dead," said the man, with no attempt to cushion the blow of his words either by adjusting his tone or softening his expression.

Just when Norman felt there was no alternative but to beat a hasty retreat to his beamer, the man looked up and invited him across the threshold.

"Would you like to come in, Mr - ?"

"Archer, Norman Archer. I believe you knew my dad."

Ferguson seemed to struggle with that concept, but he waddled through to the kitchen. Archer, in pursuit, was struck by the man's comic gait. The door to the drawing room was open, revealing a collection of musical instruments: piano, two guitars, a violin and saxophone. How strange that such a chaotic house should be home to so many expensive items.

"You and your wife holidayed in his property – River View Cottage. Up at Scarborough. It was…it was quite a traumatic time, I believe."

Ferguson carried on moving about the room, clearing away some pots, tidying a chair under the table.

"I'm afraid the cottage burned down shortly after your stay there," Archer blurted out.

Ferguson stopped dead in his tracks, turned round and spoke to Norman through pursed lips.

"Do you drink tea or would you like a beer?"

Norman looked at the disgusting state of the kitchen and although he was dry-mouthed and would have welcomed a drink, he put safety first. Here was a man who had gone to pieces, he thought. Hygiene would not be top of his list.

"I just had a coffee on the motorway, thanks," he lied.

Ferguson constantly licked his lips and acted like he was in something of a drugged state, but Norman Archer thought it might have been triggered by the terrible information he had just imparted. He returned to his theme, keen to recruit Ferguson's sympathy.

"The fire was started by some nutter who took the cottage after you and your missus. You were the last people to stay in it as it was."

"Better take a seat over here," Ferguson indicated a scruffy armchair by a patio window.

Archer tried a speculative shot.

"I didn't realise when you stayed at the cottage that your wife – Mrs Ferguson – was ill."

"Oh she wasn't" Ferguson replied, "She was fine and dandy. Never a day's illness in Carmel's life. No, it was the cottage that made her ill."

Archer raised his eyebrows. "The cottage? How exactly?"

"Did your dad tell you about that day?"

"Not really," Archer blagged, (he had never even seen his father to speak about the subject).

"You should have a talk with him about it."

Once more he wiped his lips on the back of his hand as though to say 'that's my final word'. But Norman Archer was not to be deflected from his purpose.

"That would be hard, Mr Ferguson. My dad passed away recently – stomach cancer."

Ferguson went white. Norman watched it happen; the colour visibly drained from the man's face.

"That's what got my Carmel."

Ferguson drew himself a glass of water, drank it greedily then proceeded to give Archer a full account of the séance that had taken place that day. How his wife's voice had changed and how she taken on multiple personalities before morphing into the Reverend Godfrey Merryweather and from that how they had learned about the true origins of the cottage.

"Do you mind if I scribble all that down?" Archer asked, producing a notebook and pen.

Surprise registered on Ferguson's face but 'Carry on' he said in a quiet voice.

"Carmel passed out at the end of the seance. That was nothing remarkable. That often happened when she did consultations. It's intense work when she focuses on a distressed atmosphere… I mean it *was* intense work when she *focused*."

He paused, as though to take in one more time the fact that his wife had passed on. After taking a final sip of water, he continued.

"But when she came round that day, she constantly complained about a dull ache within her stomach. It was there the whole journey home. I asked her to describe it. 'Like nothing I've known before' she said.

"Its intensity came and went for the next 'I-don't-know-how-many' weeks, but it never completely went away. She kept complaining about it, but wouldn't go to the doctor. Till she couldn't take anymore. One day they took her in for all the tests. Kept her in hospital overnight. It came out that she had the big c. They let her home and she never left the house again." This last sentence was said with the deepest gravity and Archer stopped scribbling so he could give it due attention before responding.

"My dad suffered too," Archer said, wanting to impart the impression that he had been close to his father.

Ferguson nodded. "And did he get *visited* during his last days – your dad?"

"Visited? What do you mean by 'visited'?"

"Visited by another. Carmel was. Some nights I would sit with her in her bedroom. She was afraid, see? She told me more than once that she was woken by something she couldn't describe, but I never saw a thing… until one night we both fell asleep and I woke up suddenly. I seemed to get some kind of warning. She stayed sound asleep but I was awake enough to see it bending over her. God knows what it was, but it put the fear up me."

"So do you know what it was?" Norman asked. "Could it have been someone who'd broken in the house – a burglar, maybe?"

"Nothing like that. It wasn't a person at all."

"Can you describe it then, this thing?" Norman asked, trying hard to conceal his inappropriate excitement. This, after all, was the kind of stuff he was after.

"Not well, I can't, but the main thing about it was its colour, a strange shade of almost luminous blue."

"But did it look like a man? Or was it a . . . a beast of some kind?"

"Well, it kept changing shape. It had a face, I think, but the face never looked up. Carmel said that too. 'It's always looking at the ground' she would say, 'or its own feet'."

"So if it was a person, was it man or woman?"

"That's just it" Ferguson said, "You couldn't tell and I don't think you were meant to. It was a thing and that's all I could say."

"Was it just a face or did it have a body?"

"Oh no. Not what you or I would call a body. It was just, like, a disembodied head and face and it could float around the room."

"Float around the room? So how did it finally disappear?"

"Vanished into thin air like it was a vapour that just disappeared. You could see it one minute then you couldn't."

"Did your wife give you any clue as to what she thought it might be?"

"Oh yes. Even towards the end, when she was deep into the morphine, she said the same. 'One of the undead from the crypt' was how she described it."

"I can't make head nor tail of this."

“What Carmel can do – could do – was transform herself into different personalities. They inhabited her body. I told you she became the vicar from hundreds of years ago that day at your father’s house. He was the vicar of St Mary’s church at the time of the plague… in the 1600’s. As well as ministering to his flock, he worked among the dead and dying.

“The bricks and casement windows at River View were originally part of the crypt – where the dead and dying had been stored, away from the living.

“When Carmel manifested as Merryweather she retained a memory of his persona after she emerged from the spirit state. She became Carmel again, but she could accurately recall an hour or so earlier when she had been Merryweather. Only for a brief while, you understand. In between holding her stomach with the pain, she talked about it in the taxi going to the railway station.”

“And what did she tell you?”

“About the plague. It was unbelievable. She told it me like she was actually there. She was speaking as the vicar see, not as Carmel. She told me how it started as a terrible pain in people’s insides – like something was gnawing away at them…”

“That must have been frightening…”

“But there was worse to come. She said - he said - that a body started to turn blue, like the blood was draining out of them. The closer they got to death the bluer they turned and, at the end, before their final breath, each one would be clutching at his or her stomach in agony.”

“Was that it? Was there anything else?”

"She told me Merryweather was seized by guilt because he became convinced that he had assisted the grave digger in burying a living person wrapped in a cloth. She understood how he woke often in the middle of the night sensing that he had shovelled dirt on a body in the ground."

"But he was the minister. How could that be?"

"The dead and the dying lay on the floor next to one another in the church. Merryweather had misunderstood the gravedigger's instruction and put the wrong body in the hole."

"What a terrible fate," Archer said, "I couldn't think of a worse."

"In Victorian times the rich lived in fear of being buried alive, you know," Ferguson said, "they were paranoid about it. They used to pay for a tube to be installed from the coffin to the surface of the grave."

"But they would still starve to death…"

"Not if they used the tube to shout for help."

There was a lengthy silence. For Archer it was an embarrassing one. He had all the information he needed so a swift exit was now his primary target.

"Well, thanks for the chat. I'm so sorry about your wife. I'd better be on my way. More snow according to the weather forecast."

"So they say."

Archer stood up and shuffled towards the door.

"Mr Archer…you didn't tell me what you came for."

"What I came for?"

"You've made the long journey from North Yorkshire to Birmingham in a snowstorm. There must have been a reason."

Archer's embarrassment increased. He was reluctant to make any disclosure to this stranger. Fortunately for him he saw some wiggle room.

"I told you at the beginning. I wanted to talk to your wife about the ruin of the cottage I inherited from dad. I knew some crazy things happened before the fire and I wanted to get a full picture."

"But you said it was burned to the ground. What can you do with it now?"

"Some older parts of the building survived. I wanted to start again with it, but word in the village is not good. The council are on my back. I have to weigh up my options."

"If it was me, I'd walk away from it," Ferguson said.

"Well, that's one of the options."

But Norman Archer knew that was not the option he would take.

"Do you miss her?" he asked the forlorn figure who stood in the doorway as he looked back down the length of the garden path.

"Terribly. Do you know one of the sad things I've done? I've sprayed her favourite perfume around the bedroom. As I fall asleep I can fool myself she's still there."

Not given to sentiment, Archer felt the man's misery as though it was his own.

"You know Carmel was big on family trees. Her own was fascinating. She had a great grandmother – sometime back in the 1700's – she reckoned she was the last woman in Wales to be hanged for witchcraft."

"Really?"

"She said that was probably were her powers came from in the first place. Maybe even before that. I never knew her be wrong about a person. If she said someone was not to be trusted, I knew I could rely on that."

"Incredible. I never heard of someone with a power like that."

"That was my Carmel."

Ferguson shuffled through the melting snow, accompanying him to his car despite Norman's continued protestations. He insisted on shaking hands and wished him good luck.

Barely five minutes down the road Norman pulled into a parking area, took out his pad and pen and scribbled furiously details he had felt it was inappropriate to record while Ferguson had been recounting his wife's final days.

He had got more than enough out of the trip south to bolster his ideas of what to do next. As tricky as the drive home was in the motorway slush and the dancing snowflakes, his attention was on his master plan for River View Cottage or, as he had decided it was to be called from hereon, Golgotha.

*

CHAPTER TWELVE: *The Tour Guide's Tale*

St Mary's, the church from which I came, is now but a distant memory. These days my windows and doors are of high-strength plastic and my walls have cavities that hold a thousand secrets. High-tensile steel lines my every nook and cranny. In my ceilings are ultra-sensitive sprinklers which will dampen even the hint of a flame. Despite all the foot traffic that passes through my rooms, no one ever smokes within my walls.

SMOKING STRICTLY PROHIBITED

The stonework that remains from my earliest days has been scrubbed and industrially treated and reset with the utmost care. Renovated. This is the part that enables the boast that 'Golgotha is made up of a significant section of the original building'.

The lavish brochure that most visitors purchase tells them that this entrance area is constructed from stone which was taken from a church built as long ago as the 15th century.

This stone formed the crypt of St Mary's church and served as a holding chamber for the dead and dying during the days when the bubonic plague was rampant in this part of England. The late Carmel Ferguson, a medium of note, claimed that an evil force was constantly present within that part of the build. Although these original stones were severely damaged by the recent fire they have been lovingly restored by modern craftsmen.

The front garden, through which visitors pass, contains a mock Victorian style grave. It was constructed on the site of the old laburnum tree. The replica headstone informs the client that here lie the remains of the builder of this cottage who was murdered most brutally at the hands of his architect. Of course Ashcroft's remains are not in this place, they are in the village graveyard, but that is not the point.

Helped by his meeting with Robert Ferguson, Norman Archer commissioned a reconstruction of how the upper strata of Victorian society buried its dead. Ashcroft's grave is a mere folly, but it adds to the authenticity of the visitor's experience.

The twisted oak tree was not felled. Its eccentric shape appealed to Norman. Enquiries had revealed no similar trees within a hundred miles.

"It adds to the ambience of the place," he declared, "eccentricity is to be encouraged."

Ironically, he had no clue about its origin or the boy that lay beneath; simply thought it a freak of nature.

After pondering on such morbid niceties, a mosaic path leads the visitor round the side of the house to the point of entry.

'Beware flying slates' a sign warns at one point. This explanation of Monse's untimely end is in the guide book.

Edwin Monse, reputedly a good friend of the famed thespian Sir Henry Irving, died here in a freak occurrence. A slate flew off the house's roof and embedded itself in his head.

Where the outhouse was, scene of Joan Groves' final moments, is the place that patrons pay their entry fee.

Feel the chill says a neat metallic plate above the door, though it is not clear whether it is a question or a definitive statement.

Now there is a covered way that leads them into the Leonard Broome Room of Terror. Here, according to the guide book, were spent the final minutes of the famous child-killer. Set up on an oak table, visitors can peruse one of two leather-bound versions of *The Candelight Killer,* the edited confessions of a murderer who once resided within these walls. They can spend a few moments dwelling upon the awfulness of a satanic man, a killer who terrorised families in the north of England.

In his book, Broome told the world that his real name was Leonid Bromski. That his father, a mad Russian Jew, had treated him abominably, chaining him up like a dog, feeding him in a kennel. Only occasionally had he allowed him to be treated like a son should be.

'No wonder I hated my own father enough to kill him' he declared, 'though I will never tell where his remains are. He does not deserve to be remembered.'

Taken from that confessional book and printed upon the wall of this room are the words of William Shakespeare. Leonard Broome said within his confession that it was while studying *MacBeth* at school he had come to realise the profundity of the bard's words about the fragility of life.

Tomorrow and tomorrow and tomorrow,
Creeps in this pretty pace from day to day,
To the last syllable of recorded time;
And all our yesterday's have lighted fools
The way to dusty death. Out, out, brief candle!

Life's but a walking shadow, a poor player
That struts and frets his hour upon the stage,
And then is heard no more; it is a tale
Told by an idiot, full of sound and fury,
Signifying nothing.

In *The Candlelight Killer* the author made much of how he should be revered for saving so many lives from endless pain. Implicit in such a declaration was a condemnation of his own tortured existence.

"I only ever took the lives of those whose ultimate fate was days full of desperation and drudgery. They were the children of the destitute, the degraded, the despondent; destined for a life that 'signified nothing.'

"You would be mistaken to think my acts of murder were cruel and heartless. I was blessed with the power to foretell the fate of those whose lives I snuffed out. Their lives would have been humdrum and misery-ridden. I saved them from that.

"Which is crueller, to stand and watch and do nothing as empty meaningless young lives develop into tortured adulthoods or to take action through foresight and compassion to end needless suffering?"

Broome proclaimed himself a new existentialist and spent pages and pages of his book reflecting upon the pointlessness of existence. Only those who could follow their dreams and those who were the ultimate hedonists could justify their lives, he said.

The world at large was appalled by Broome's actions and his twisted thinking, although a number of child psychologists pointed out that damage done in the first years of childhood is serious collateral damage. The real monster of the piece, they said, was Leonid's father.

Of course, there were those warped individuals who pored over his writings and saw him as some kind of prophet worthy of a latter-day cult. A London company came up with a t-shirt that portrayed Broome as an icon; his face framed by burning candles.

There were the doubters too: those who believed the fire that consumed the cottage was a deliberate ploy by Broome so that he could cover his tracks and make an elaborate escape. Broome was out there, these would-be disciples said, and the skull that had been discovered in the fire-ravaged building had been another of Broome's victims, planted by him with the intention of deceiving the police.

In place of the casement windows, which were destroyed in the fire, is a tiny chapel of rest in which Broome's victims can be remembered in quietude. This is set aside for those who are overcome by grief during their Golgotha Experience. Visitors are asked to respect the feelings of those who wish to spend a few moments in quiet prayer.

Staying on the ground floor and moving towards the new stairwell, the visitors can see a stain upon the floor. Although this stain has been renewed by modern technology, the book tells visitors that it was indelible for over a century.

'Here be the spot' says the sign and the book goes on to tell visitors that this very mark was where Austin Lincoln, the architect of the original house, felled his paymaster with a blow from a hammer. Here also is the place where, years later, the gardener's son breathed his last and a family became cursed.

Ashcroft's killer, Austin Lincoln, they will learn, went on to be the only sentenced murderer in Salford jail to actually survive the hangman's noose, but even he came back to die at the scene of his crime, a victim of Golgotha's curse.

Upstairs in the smallest bedroom is a miracle of modern science. Visitors are asked to remain stock still for a few seconds, which causes a hologram to light up.

A brilliant illusion of cornflower blue lights up the room, night or day, and this indefinable, unnamed vision breeds fear into hearts and minds. (No young person under the age of 16 is allowed entry to this part of the building. A steward ensures the house rules are observed).

A well-positioned tour guide tells the clientele that for many years people in the house were terrorised by a similar blue indefinable form that moved through the rooms.

The guide's carefully rehearsed speech echoes round the building on a daily basis. The man is an out of work actor and his script is an amalgam of fact and fiction.

"What was that blue shape?" he will say to the punters at a moment that catches them unawares, but then proceeds to answer his own question.

"No one can be sure," he goes on in sepulchral tones, "but during the plague years it was not uncommon for the dying to be buried before they had breathed their last."

"Such was the fear of this possibility in Victorian times that the rich would purchase a tube linking the corpse in the coffin with the surface. The victim who had been mistaken for dead could then breathe and shout for help. You see, a doctor's skill, his ability to make a definitive decision on whether or not a person was dead, was not as clear-cut as we expect it to be in today's world."

There is at this point usually a sharp pronounced intake of breath as the more credulous among the tour party imagine the awfulness of such a fate.

After a brief pause for effect, the out of work actor continues with his peroration.

"It is thought that the moonlight reflected the victim's face in the days that this part of the building was a church crypt. If you were unfortunate enough to be visited by this vision in blue then you were cursed. Indeed, we know of at least two people within the last 20 years who have suffered such a fate… And they are no longer with us today."

"Ladies and gentleman" he will say, "We take our houses for granted. We think of them just as wood and steel, bricks and plaster, glass and concrete. And yet Golgotha bears testimony to the fact that the buildings in which we dwell are so much more than mere materials and objects devoid of emotional investment."

Oh he's good. He's very good. His script is carefully layered. It has been written by an expert team, cobbled together by Norman Archer, the man who spotted the niche in the market. The tour guide's pauses are in all the right places. The dramatic effects are worked to perfection, all carefully rehearsed. Golgotha has become a legend, a clever mix of fact and fiction, marketed with cunning and clear vision.

***

Overnight Special

Have you ever considered spending the night in a haunted house? It is the ultimate challenge. The ghosts of Golgotha house are the stuff of legend. Spend the whole night in a group of four on a special rate - £200 including a supernatural supper, (7pm to 7am), and your own overnight tour guide.

Cameras, tape recorders plus specialist equipment allowed.

Strictly No Alcohol

***

I am a far cry from the house that once I was. Instead of resonating to everyday life and human drama, I am an empty shell composed of manmade materials and the plasticity of a re-constructed past.

I often reflect on the flame that destroyed so much of my past. Was it some kind of purifying fire that purged my walls of all voices and resonances from the past that were trapped within?

They say that glass cries. Over the years, gravity pulls the atoms earthward and the tears create tracks, they say. Such is the power of urban myth.

Now my windows are of a reinforced plastic: a material more suited to the modern age. Even if once I cried, I will never cry again.

At the new beginning, before I was rebuilt, there had been a meeting. There were three of them: Norman, his mother and Valentine Huntley. Huntley was a solicitor that Norman had latched onto at the Chamber of Commerce. The man claimed his clan had lived in the area since Neolithic Man.

"Don't be an arse, Val. No one goes that far back."

"Okay, Norman, I may be exaggerating to prove a point, but 'Daddy' says we were landed gentry and he's got the family tree to prove it."

Although he took this with a pinch of salt, Norman was aware that Valentine could be useful if things worked out. But those roots were not as important as the fact that the solicitor had plenty of loot and was prepared to splash some of it in Norman's direction. He was the only one in that coterie of commercial cretins who would run with what everyone else had labelled Norman's madcap scheme.

So they had stood together a year earlier in a River View Cotaage that was little more than a burnt out bombsite of a place, held together with spit, tape and hope.

Margaret Archer spoke first.

"So hopefully you are now going to tell me what exactly this pet project is about, Norman. Why's it all been so hush-hush?"

"Because, mother, it can make us a lot of money, but there will be opposition. You know how quickly passions are aroused when money's about."

"Opposition from who?"

Huntley could answer that one. "Locals, Margaret. Town council. Parish council. Anybody who thinks they're being put out. Police too. Probably fearing the worst from the kind of riff-raff our project might attract."

Norman jumped in defensively at that. "It won't attract riff-raff. We're going to do this tastefully. The worst we can expect is some controversy because we are creating something that no one ever tried before. We are pathfinders."

Margaret gulped in air like it was all too much for her.

"So for God's sake, Norman, give me some detail. Tell me what it's about."

"I'm turning River View Cottage from a holiday house into a themed house."

"Theme house? Country crafts and local history sort of thing? You think that will make you a pile of money?"

"The theme, dear mother, is the supernatural."

"Ghosts?"

Huntley took up the reins. "Look at River View's past, Margaret. It's littered with dead bodies, mysterious characters and ruined relationships. The stuff of legend and folklore."

"How do you know that, both of you?"

"Because, dear mother, I did a load of research. You would be amazed. This is so much more than an ordinary house. It deserves to be celebrated."

But Margaret was not so easily enthused. “And you will cash in on this how? ‘Come and buy your bundle of misery here?’”

That brought out the entrepreneur in Huntley. Waving his hands extravagantly, like some eccentric professor, he explained that he and Norman would convert River View Cottage into ‘a focus of fear.’

“Yes, we’ll turn it into a haunted house, but one that is controlled so people will be secure with the experience and not scarred by it,” Norman added.

Norman nodded approvingly at his own good sense. “What we don’t have is a name for the house.”

“Why not ‘the haunted house’,” Margaret suggested.

“Lacks imagination, mother. Makes it sound like a fairground attraction.”

“I came up with Spookytooth,” said Huntley, wearing a wide grin.

But Norman had been waiting his moment. He was not short of ideas. Last night he had come up with what he thought was a surefire winner. His expression intensified.

“What about … Golgotha?”

“Golgotha?” Huntley parroted back, a note of disbelief in his voice.

“Golgotha? What’s that supposed to mean?” Margaret Archer asked.

“The place of the skull. Think about it. A skull, that’s all we found of Broome after the fire.”

“Wasn’t Golgotha where Christ was crucified?” Margaret asked.

"Exactly," Norman responded, warming to his own proposal "and it has 'goth' in the middle. Think of all the resonances."

"It does have a certain *je ne sais quoi.* I believe that Golgotha is a word they use these days to describe a place where bad things have happened," Huntley admitted.

"I must be mad to go along with this," Margaret Archer said, looking up through the non-existent ceiling.

"But you will, mother, won't you?" Norman asked with the enthusiasm of a puppy.

"I suppose."

And that was how I came to be reborn.

The four of them were very young; loquacious, rambunctious even. To them the whole project of an overnight stay in a haunted house had been triggered by a bet made at the rugby club. Owen Hamshaw had been overheard in the rugby club bar floating the idea to any first teamers in the vicinity.

"My grandad's always gone on about it – it's near the river. Says it was called River View Cottage in his day. Some bloke named Norman Archer owns it now. He's turned it into a kind of theme house. The dare is to spend a night in it. What about a few of you joining me, doing it as a charity thing? Raise money for a good cause."

Three of the rowdy team-mates Owen had been drinking with stuck hands up in the air and vowed their allegiance to the cause. The raucous air was full of bonhomie and a 'can do' spirit emanated from the party.

"When do we go for it?" one of the volunteers asked.

“The sooner the better” Owen told them, “but we’ll need to raise the overnight fee - £200.”

Things went distinctly quiet as that information sank in.

“So let me get this right” asked Graeme, one of the now not so enthusiastic volunteers, “we stump up £200 in cash to spend the night in a dump that will scare our bollocks off?”

“That’s a bit over the top,” Owen said. “Think of it as a charity gig. We get sponsored per hour that we last it out.”

The noise frequency in the immediate vicinity, previously a riot of yells and laughter, dropped several notches.

Across the room, someone had been listening in.

“I’ll pay your entrance money and give you back double the amount for charity if you can last the full 12 hours. You can give the money to children in need,” the club president told them, “as long as you tell the media that you were sponsored by Fenby Fine Furnishings.”

All eyes were diverted across the room to the club president alias Ally Fenby, chief executive of FFF. Overweight and smug, a man who emphasised the ex in ex rugby player, Fenby smiled with the confidence of a man who knows that money talks.

This was turning into a worthwhile project. On the periphery of the group, propping up the bar was the club coach, a man who had seen it all and wore a tee-shirt advertising the fact.

“You lot make me laugh. You’re like young thrushes” he interjected, “all gob and arsehole. Not one of you would last five minutes if you were in there on your own. See a ghost? You're more likely to see a pink elephant."

"So you're saying there's no such things as ghosts, but if there were we'd run off like a load of pussies?" Owen Hamshaw asked him.

Owen's blood was fired by the coach's cynicism. He and his three fellow recruits were up for almost anything. The four of them were considered 'wild young things', having won their cred by doing over a hotel room last year on the club trip to Twickenham.

"Done" said Owen, reaching out to shake Fenby's hand, "we'll take your money and show the world what we're made of."

In turn, the other three stepped forward to seal the deal by shaking the president's hand.

There was a lengthy silence as it sunk in just what the group had undertaken.

"This was the place that Leonard Broome made his last stand," Owen told them.

"Who the hell's Leonard Broome?" asked Danny Boyes.

"Don't you read the papers? Child killer. Killed himself in that house," Graeme, the junior of the group, informed him.

"Do we have to stay awake all night?" Christian asked.

"That would be no fun," Danny told him, "sleeping through it, I mean. If we see a ghost I want to be able to tell people about it."

"Here's what we do," Owen declared, assuming the mantle of leadership. "I'll bring a wine glass and all the letters of the alphabet. We'll set up a Ouija board…and see if we can contact him."

"Him?" asked Christian.

"Broome, ya plonker," Graeme told him. "If that place is haunted, it's got to be his ghost in there, hasn't it?"

"Best if we take a bit of booze," Danny said, thinking as usual that beer was the best way to deal with any misgivings.

"Booze is against the house rules," Owen told him, "but we do get a supper."

"Who's to know if we smuggle in a bit of booze?"

"They have a man staying the night with you – security."

"We'll bribe him. Should be easy. These people are paid peanuts. Flash the cash and he'll turn a blind eye. They all do."

In truth Owen was the only one who took the challenge seriously. His family had managed the Cock and Feathers for at least 150 years that he knew of. When he had told them about the project a few days earlier his father and grandfather had told him not to be so soft.

"Ghost hunting at your age…"

"Don't meddle with the devil," said granddad, as if he was blessed with the wisdom of age.

"But we'll get sponsorship and raise loads for charity."

"Don't go getting yourself into more trouble…like last time" said his father, referring to the hullabaloo that followed Owen's trip to London a year earlier when the hotel room had been seriously trashed.

"It's not like I'm on my own, dad" Owen told them, "there are three other guys from the rugby club. C'mon, it's only a bit of fun and it's all in a good cause. Fenby, the president, says he'll give us four hundred for children in need."

Grandad looked on sanguinely.

"We have a generation of people who seem to think fear is fun," he told anyone who cared to listen, "they might think differently if they'd fought in a war."

*

CHAPTER THIRTEEN: *The Watchman's Tale*

Norman Archer's man could hardly be thought of as a security guard. He was in his fifties, tall, wispy ginger hair gathered in a halo round his crown making him look monk-like. He was only too glad of the opportunity to earn some 'pin money' by doing a nightshift. Locally-based, he had once owned a small stone yard and building company, but that had gone bust three years ago and the pennies were short. Answering an ad in the local paper, he was signed up by Norman Archer because of his local knowledge.

"Family have lived round here for longer than I care to remember, Mr Archer."

"So you know Golgotha?"

"Well, of course I knew it as River View Cottage, but you've given it a new name."

"And do you like it – the new name?"

That was a tough question to answer. He hated it, but needed the job fairly desperately.

"Has a very dramatic ring to it."

"Good, I wanted it to have."

The job was modest money, but beggars could not be choosers. This time a year ago, he had had three men in his employ, but now he was swimming in debt. Times were tough. A man of his years had little hope of work in such proximity to home. Instinctively he disliked Archer, but pride was an unaffordable luxury. He would take the man's money.

He sat now in the small entrance hall, apprehensive about the coming night party. He feared they might prove a raucous ungovernable mob, having heard they were a bunch of rugby players. Kids these days. Even his own son could prove a handful and he was nearer 30 than 20.

The supernatural supper for four, brought by taxi from a local kitchen, had arrived half an hour ago and he was keeping it warm in the oven.

Suddenly there was a staccato burst of thumping on the front door. His heart hammered in his chest, betraying the true state of his confidence. Loud giggling in the background. The noise of youths in a ruck. Trouble and mayhem. All his worst fears were being confirmed.

Nonplussed, he opened the door, trying his best to deceive, to appear cool, calm and collected. On the positive side, he had done this watch a few times and he was used to meeting all sorts. Usually they came in mixed sex groups with an air of nervous adventure about them. He had managed mixed groups like that with ease, even helped contribute to the creepy atmosphere his employer wanted. But he sensed that this lot were a different kind of challenge.

The four flushed faces that met him once he opened the front door, (the creak was realistic but electronically triggered in fact), were already full of beer. They were slightly older than expected and he felt his apprehension levels lift. Rather than a simple overnight watch job, this was clearly a situation that would require some involvement, intervention even.

“That door seriously needs oiling” one of them said. The guard just chuckled politely; he didn’t want to give the game away.

He looked down at the paperwork in his hand and addressed all four men in search of a leader. “Mr Hamshaw?”

“Aye, that’s me.”

“I take it you’re the man in charge; can you sign here?”

“Course I can, chief.”

He tried his best to muster a matey we’re-all-in-this-together tone.

“Come in and make yourselves comfortable.”

Make them at home; no sense in early aggravation.

“Your supper is in the oven. Get yourselves organised round this table and I’ll serve you up.”

The table was small and the chairs of the fold-up variety, but the food looked promising enough.

“There is a complimentary bottle of non-alcohol wine,” he told them.

They chuckled with good humour and at that point he was hopeful that the evening might pass without incident.

The room was consumed with the busy sound of eating: the clanking of cutlery, the tinkle of pots, slurping and sounds of approval as the four of them reduced the feast to a few scraps.

When the meal was over the night watchman asked them to put away their chairs which he said he would remove to an upstairs bedroom.

“There’s no need” said Owen, “we have a plan that involves them.”

"No problem."

"We've all brought sleeping bags for later, like the leaflet asked us to," Owen informed him.

"So would you like me to get the foam mattresses out?"

"Foam? Oh aye. Keep it as bubbly as possible and bring on the dancing girls," said the one named Christian.

Now Danny took up the chat. He wasn't far gone, but there was a distinct slur to his speech for they had spent some time working up their courage in Owen's dad's pub, the Cock and Feathers.

"Is it all right if we bring in a few beers? They're in the boot of Owen's car down the lane."

"Sorry, I have to remind you - no alcohol. They're the rules."

Danny took out his wallet and flicked a finger at the note compartment.

"Would a bit of persuasion be in order?"

"Definitely not," the night watchman insisted, "no alcohol, no flames, no fire."

"Forgive me for saying this," Graeme jumped in, "but there's not a lot you could do about it if we just went ahead."

"I could make a phone call," the night watchman said, sounding a lot more confident than he felt.

"Lads, lads, calm down – all this aggro," said Owen, taking control. "The man's got a job to do, he doesn't need funny beggars."

Things went quiet and the four of them slumped into the easy chairs, focused on making themselves comfortable for the evening. The conversation, when it started, was of rugby and women and the trivial things that young men laugh about.

Down the centuries all manner of persons have lived within my confines, but now I glimpsed modern youth and his arrogant self at work. To these four, already lubricated by drink, the history of this building was obscured. The brochure told them that I was once a place of worship, but that was remote to them and not a cause for respect, only a standing joke.

In days gone by I had held memories and echoes that impressed those who were sensitive, but now I was characterless, a fairground attraction. Broome's inferno had destroyed me as thoroughly as he had decimated the families whose children he had taken.

The Archers, father and son, had taken their toll on my personality too. Cleansing and restoring scorched bricks, subverting my purpose; they had done nothing to re-install my history, to give me dignity.

For the persons of this modern day and age, houses are not built to hold history. Men have found ways to construct on sand, to bridge on water, to defy the laws of physics. Houses are built for the here and now, instant structures existing to hold the present with little thought for the future. As for the past, it is either warehoused or trashed.

Before the punters from the rugby club could fulfil their wishes, the security man needed to be dealt with.

"Our plan is to do the Ouija. Is that all right with you if we go ahead?" Owen asked him.

"The Ouija?"

"It's like a board game, to get in touch with the spirit world," Owen answered.

"Do as you like so long as it's within the rules," the man said in a resigned manner, then added "You pays your money and you takes your chance."

"One other thing" Owen said, "in the morning we'll need you to sign a letter for us, to say we lasted the night. It's for charity, see?"

"A good thing, supporting a charity. Of course I'll sign. My pleasure."

There was much rearranging of furniture as the four of them pushed the easy chairs into the corner of the room, cleared the makeshift dining table and returned to the folding chairs.

Out of a small backpack he carried, Owen Hamshaw took the 26 letters of the alphabet he had created on cards plus two bearing the words 'yes' and 'no. These he spread round the table in a circle, taking pains to ensure the symmetry. Finally, he took the glass out of his pack, spat in it and then rubbed it clean with the flap of his shirt.

"Here's the wine glass, lads. Now, who's gonna ask the first question?"

Graeme raised his hand, like the little lad he was. He looked so young he might have left school yesterday.

The night watchman was surprised that they felt no embarrassment at his continued presence.

"Okay, everybody, fingers on the wine glass," said Owen. He had inverted the glass so that the fingers could rest on the base and the rim slid smoothly along the table top. When the murmurs had ceased he nodded in Graeme's direction.

Graeme licked his lips. Beads of sweat stood out on his forehead. There had always been a studied seriousness about Graeme. He spoke now in sepulchral tones.

"Leonard Broome, are you present in this room?"

Christian burst out laughing, destroying the tension.

"Ha, he's a poet and he don't even know it."

"What?" a mystified Graeme asked.

"Broome and room" Christian repeated.

"Sssshhhh!" everyone else demanded.

"You have to take it seriously," Owen pleaded. "He'll never turn up if we just mess about." At that he turned to the security man, "Isn't that right?"

He nodded weakly. "Don't ask me, mate. You lot are going places I've never been."

"I mean" says Owen to the man, "you must have witnessed plenty of weirdos spending nights here in the time you've worked here as a watchman."

"Never seen anyone do the Ouija" the man said truthfully.

"Do you think the ghost of Leonard Broome is in this building?" Graeme asked with naïve intensity.

"Search me," the man said.

"Ah, so you don't believe in ghosts," said Danny.

"I never said that."

"Look" said Christian, "Just tell us. Is this haunted house thing a con? All this stuff," he said flinging out his arms to indicate the house, "Broome, the man they couldn't hang, the drowning boy who died in a pool of blood, the plague victims: is it just a wind-up?"

"I know for sure some of it's true."

At that he had them. They came under his spell like kids before a persuasive teacher in a primary classroom.

"And how do you know that?" asked Owen.

The man turned round on Owen sharply. "You should know as well as me, young man. Your family come from this village."

"Meaning what?"

"Ask your granddad what he knows about this place in the days when it was River View Cottage."

"You say that like you come from round here too."

"Oh I do. Name's Ashcroft, William Ashcroft."

"Should that mean anything to me?"

"It was my family many moons ago that built this house."

"So was it a relative of yours that was killed by 'the man they couldn't hang'?"

"It was that. My great great granddad, I believe."

"So is that why you're doing this – do you have shares in this place?"

Ashcroft chuckled.

"No. This is just a part-time job to help me tick over. Need a bit of pocket money these days."

An impatient Graeme jumped in. "Look, you lot, are we doing this Ouija thing or not?"

In a quiet voice, welcoming the opportunity to escape the pressure, Ashcroft said "Why don't I take myself upstairs?"

"No, you're all right to stay," Owen said.

"If I go upstairs I won't put you off your Ouija. You can have your fun, no worries. You might feel self-conscious if I'm around or you might think I'm manipulating things."

"Good idea to leave us on our own," said Danny, "I'm nipping out for a fag first though."

Of course, the night watchman, Ashcroft, must have known what they were up to. He was no fool. The lad who was 'nipping out' was the one who had tried to soften him up about alcohol. It was clearly part of a plan to smuggle in some booze. What did he care? Let them get on with it. He was confident that he could keep these lads under control…now that he knew one of them was Hamshaw's lad. Ashcroft's stock was good at the Cock and Feathers. If the worst came to the worst a well-placed phone call would get some support.

While they were distracted, he nipped up the stairs. In the upstairs room he had set aside a couch on which he could stretch out. He took out his paper and folded it at the crossword. He was quite comfortable up there on his own. No thoughts of supernatural beings or atmospheres of evil intruded on his thoughts. He thought the whole thing a sham, but what did it matter as long as no one got hurt?

Danny returned with a heavy cardboard box of bottled beers. Christian made a big thing of shushing everybody then used his penknife to lever the tops off four beers. The company retired to the easy chairs and for some time there was the hum of conversation punctuated by bursts of silence as beer was imbibed. They talked of loose women, lousy bosses and pointless work and their frustrations with the everyday world. Soon the alcohol eased their moods and laughter flowed.

It was Owen who brought them back to the board. He had assembled them for a project and he wasn't going to let it slip away.

"I've got a better idea than asking a dumb question about whether Broome is here," Owen said. "All put your index fingers on the wineglass."

They complied. He waited a minute for a hush to fall on the group.

"How many people are in this house?" he asked.

"Count for yourself," Christian burst out, but Owen put a finger to his lips. "It's the glass I'm asking, not you, daft boy."

For a few seconds there was nothing, but, amazingly, the four young men controlled their nervous excitement. Then, gradually, unbelievably, the glass stuttered into life. It crawled across the table, spelling out S – I – X.

"Six?" Christian protested, "But there are only four of us."

"Then there's the bloke upstairs," Danny reminded him, "the night watchman."

"Okay, that's five."

The group went silent and looked at each other across the table.

The truth dawned on them. Hamshaw's boy spoke it first. "*It's* counting itself. Us five and *it*. That's six."

"Is *it* really in here with us?" asked Danny, now moving in to the credulous camp.

"No" said Christian, "I read that Ouija is nothing to do with ghosts. It's us doing it. All of us."

"Not me" protested Graeme, "I just rested my finger on the glass. Never tried to move a thing."

"You don't know you're doing it," said Christian, "no one cheats. It's your subconscious."

"Big word for a little boy" said Danny, taking a swig from his bottle.

Upstairs Ashcroft was tired and starting to nod off over his crossword. It had been a long day. He had spent the morning doing a plastering job. Life was like that. No regular income these days, just a steady accruing of cash to meet the bills and keep heads above water. Those kids downstairs – they would be fine. Norman Archer's almost neurotic concerns that the place would be engulfed in another fire were totally misplaced. They didn't look like arsonists to him. Let them have their bit of fun and their bottles of beer.

"Fingers back on the wineglass," Owen demanded.

Everyone had to wait for the silly laughter and the clearing of throats to end. More drink had to be taken. Danny levered the tops off four more bottles. After ten minutes, it was Owen who asserted his will on the rest. Indicating the need for silence by placing both hands palm down on the table, he then indicated Graeme with his index finger. Graeme was to be the chosen one.

Graeme twitched nervously and then took up the spotlight, the concentration etched upon his forehead. The words, when they came, hung in the air like a Biblical command.

"Is-Leonard-Broome-present?"

The other three stared at him as though he was out of his mind. Doubt spread across even Owen's features.

The glass lurched across to 'Yes' and came to an abrupt halt.

Lots of lip-licking accompanied by manic stares; nervous glances towards the stairwell.

Graeme was hooked line and sinker now. Nothing could interrupt his dedication or pursuit of the terrible truth. "Is he present in this house?"

Once more, 'Yes'.

Owen seized on the fact that Graeme seemed to have a rapport with whatever powered the glass.

"Ask him, ask him if he died in the fire," he suggested, as though only Graeme could connect.

Graeme's voice, when it came, was solemn, deliberate. "Did you die in the fire?"

This time the glass sped across to the 'No' card.

"He's not dead. He's somewhere out there," said Christian, stumbling over his words.

"The fire he started, it was probably just a trick to get the police off his back...," Danny suggested.

"So that he could continue killing little kids, become a legend serial killer."

These men-children were victims of their own wild imaginings. The centuries that I had stood as first a temple then a dwelling were long past. Now I am a mere amusement, a theme house existing only for profit and play. During the years that I have stood alongside the flowing river, I have seen humanity in all its forms.

In all that time none of the dwellers within my walls could face up to where the badness, the curse, the ultimate destiny, came from. The source of fear was identified by all as being resident within my shell and not of man's own making.

All except one: the most fearsome of them all, the one who could peer deep down into the ugliness of his soul using only the pale flickering candlelight, the one who was at once the most terrible and the most insightful, the one who these four 'punters' had identified and believed they had brought back from the dead.

"Ask him, ask him," urged Owen, "Find out whereabouts he is now. We need to know."

It took almost five minutes for every finger to return to the glass and even then they were shivering with fear.

"Whereabouts in the house are you?" Graeme asked through dry lips.

For several seconds nothing happened then the glass began to circle the table erratically. It picked up speed until it resembled a child's toy car zooming in crazy laps round the table's surface. They were in the realm of the unknown. Fear showed on the faces of the four 'players' and despite their best efforts at taming the glass's manic progress, it flew off the edge of the table and smashed upon the floor.

"Don't worry. They do that. They do that. It's part of the Ouija," Owen's voice was soaked in desperation.

Since the terrible fire, nothing had resonated within my walls. I had become safe, antiseptic, a mere entertainment. My edifice had been stripped of soul. But not now. Now I could trap their terror like a living thing.

And then it moved.

Christian was first to speak upon hearing the disturbance in the upstairs room that was separated from them only by the thinness of a modern ceiling.

"Look what you've done."

For all the beer he had drunk, Danny, the comedian, was suddenly sober and focused.

"Whose idea was it to do this? It's not right. We shouldn't meddle in things like this. It's satanic. It's…it's black magic."

The four of them were now transported outside themselves. The unthinkable had happened. They had given life to a renaissance; they had caused a most foul phoenix to rise from the ashes.

The upstairs room door rocked back against the wall and within seconds the first steps could be heard upon the wooden stairs.

Transfixed by the horror of it all, Owen was the one to whisperingly declare "It's the spirit of Leonard Broome. He's coming back."

Slowly, but quite definitely, footsteps could be heard descending the stairs. The four of them existed in a bubble of silence.

Deep within Christian a kind of courage flickered. Time and again on the rugby field, people had described him as 'gutsy', 'unafraid', 'a doer not a thinker'.

"We have to get him," he whispered hoarsely. "If we don't stop him, more kids will die."

Broome's silhouetted form was there, unmistakable and silent as it reached the bottom of the stairs.

"Ssshhh, keep quiet. He doesn't know we're here. There are four of us. We can take care of him," Owen said.

Christian looked around the room for help and his gaze settled on the empty beer bottles that littered the floor. He picked one up and brandished it like a club in one hand, balling the other hand into a fist.

"Get a bottle, everyone. Let's do him over for once and all."

Ashcroft had hardly come out of his reverie since he fell asleep doing his crossword. He knew the stairs well enough to plod down them with just half a mind on the job. There was no sense of caution for all was quiet below. The party of lads he was overseeing must have finally succumbed to sleep and from here on the night would be peaceful.

He reached the bottom step and felt a crushing blow to the skull from behind. The night lit up and the pain was beyond anything he could put into words. Bottles rained down on the delicate shell of his skull, but none of it registered for he was beyond consciousness.

"Kill the beast!"

"Cut his throat!"

"Die, dog."

And so it went on for what seemed like forever until the floor was slippery then sticky with blood. The incessant shuffle of feet, the dull clubbing of bottle on bone suddenly ceased like a clockwork machine reaching the end of its spring.

"Make sure he never kills another kid," one of them cried out.

Like his father's before him, Norman Archer's plans had been brought to a swift end by tragedy. Ashcroft's death at the hands of a hysterical group of youths and a lengthy manslaughter trial had inevitably implicated him. The prosecutor had described Golgotha as a foolhardy venture that played with people's lives and made light of their deaths.

"You have been irresponsible beyond comprehension," a silver-bearded coroner told Archer. "I cannot believe you were granted permission for such a folly. It is with the deepest conviction that I ask the powers-that-be to revoke your licence."

The four rugby-playing friends, who during the inquest made much of their intention to raise money for charity, were nevertheless found guilty of manslaughter. It proved impossible to disentangle their various roles in the killing of Ashcroft so they would all go down together.

"You acted like a mindless mob. The victim had no chance. I cannot understand how you were deaf to his shouts of pain. You are each of you reasonably educated individuals who have acted without conscience. I would remind you that conscience has been defined as God's presence in man. I will attempt to restore it to each of you by sentencing you to three years in jail; time enough to ponder deeply on your actions and about what you have done in ending a man's life."

For his part, Norman Archer received a suspended sentence and was ordered by the licensing authority to close down Golgotha. His mother and Valentine Huntley refused to associate with him further. Hadn't it been his idea all along?

"And I strongly suggest that your initial action is to remove the nameplate," Spencer the coroner told him.

The team of council men, when they came, were ruthlessly efficient. All signage was taken down; electrical wiring was restored to a proper domestic purpose; the grave and other follies were removed. The chapel of rest was turned into a lounge and all references to Leonard Broome were consigned to oblivion. A bold new window replaced the old casement windows. Being eastward-facing it gave an uninterrupted view of the river and allowed full access to the morning sun.

At last I could breathe.

Insects brought their colonies back within my walls. Vermin burrowed back into the foundations and sought cracks and crannies from which to multiply. Back came life, real life, equipped with instinct and will, devoid of fear and prejudice.

But within my portals was only silence. Wind battered the brickwork, rain and snow spattered the windows, thunder rattled the roof, but of the noise of men there was none. And it stayed like that for many years.

*

EPILOGUE

Bold and brave, Anna opened the front door, followed two strides behind by little Sammy, her brother. The two of them had run on ahead of their father and entered the building without misgiving. It was a long time since I had been a home to such childish innocence.

During their excited journey from car to house they pause briefly to take in the unexpected.

On the river bank, statuesque, stands a chestnut brown colt. The children pause only to check whether this is real life or some beautiful artefact, a cleverness designed to capture passing attention.

But no. It comes to life. Straining its fine head forward and down, it seeks out the rich grass, grass of a green so intense that it hurts their eyes. Then they know, as only children know, that everything will be all right.

That one observation is good enough for them. It is real. They bound forward, desperate to explore their new home. Their father, laden with bags, follows on behind.

"Where will we sleep, daddy?"

"Follow me upstairs and I'll show you."

Unaccountably, the girl fell asleep first. Richard expected her to chatter until the early hours, consumed by curiosity about her new situation. He took it as a good sign that she felt relaxed enough to surrender to sleep so easily.

Sammy was a different story. All the questions he would have targeted at his sister were wheeled out of the store and dangled before dad.

"Is this an old house, daddy?"

Previously, when mummy and daddy were as one, they had lived on a new estate, their detached house being not more than five years old.

"It is quite old, yes."

"Is it older than you?"

Richard stifled a chuckle. "Why, yes, it is. A lot older than me."

"Is it older than granddad?"

"Yes, older than him too. Even older than grandad's granddad."

The boy's eyes grew big as saucers then came the burning question.

"Will mummy be coming here to live with us?"

In respect, he paused before answering this time. "No, Sammy. Mummy is staying where we used to live. This is daddy's house now."

"Will you get a new mummy…I mean, wife?"

"Maybe one day, son."

"Can mummy and you still be friends?"

Richard didn't want to promise the earth. "We'll try."

"Will you tell me a story?"

"To send you to sleep?"

"That's what I meant. Make it a nice story, daddy, not a scary one."

"There's nothing to be afraid of, Sammy. There's just you, me, Anna and our new house."

“I wish mummy was here.”

“I know, but you’ll see mummy again tomorrow.”

“Good. Daddy, I love mummy.”

“I know you do, Sammy. I’m glad about that.”

“Daddy, do you love mummy?”

Richard did not like the way this was going now. He could not tell lies to his young son and here in a new house, last thing at night, was not the place to reveal hurtful truths.

“Your mummy is a wonderful lady” he said, “without her there would be no Anna and no Sammy.”

The pause that followed was big enough to hold every one of Richard’s nightmares. Then to his great relief his words did the trick.

“Daddy?”

“Yes?”

“I don’t want the story anymore. I’m ready for sleepy-byes now.”

“I’m pleased to hear that, Sammy.”

The linen rustled as Richard lifted himself off the bed and moved to the door. He looked back at his son and his heart was full of the beauty of it all.

“Goodnight, son,” he said, with a tear in his voice.

Sammy’s reply was barely audible.

“Goodnight, daddy. I like this new old house.”

***